Surrounded by Vampires!

Jeep skidded to a stop.

They were all there. The whole camp. Every single person.

They were all wearing dark glasses. They were all smiling. Behind him Jeep heard footsteps come out of the infirmary door. He looked over his shoulder. Nurse Hatchett and Martin were standing there. Nurse Hatchett had on her dark glasses, too. And she and Martin were both smiling vampire smiles.

"Stand back!" screamed Jeep. "I had garlic for dinner!"

No one spoke. No one moved. They just stood there watching Jeep.

Hungrily.

Then Dawn stepped out. She pushed her sunglasses up. Her pale face glowed in the dark. "Garlic for dinner, Jeep? I don't think so. You see, we don't serve garlic at this camp."

The other vampires came closer. Closer. He was surrounded on every side. He pulled the collar of his shirt up. He put up his fists. He closed his eyes.

"You'll never take me alive!" he cried.

Other Skylark Books you won't want to miss!

GRAVEYARD SCHOOL

Camp Dracula

Tom B. Stone

A SKYLARK BOOK

Toronto   New York   London   Sydney   Auckland

RL 3.6, 008–012

CAMP DRACULA

A Skylark Book / May 1995

Skylark Books is a registered trademark of Bantam Books,
a division of Bantam Doubleday Dell Publishing Group, Inc.
Registered in U.S. Patent and Trademark Office and elsewhere.

Graveyard School™ is a registered trademark of
Bantam Doubleday Dell Publishing Group, Inc.

ISBN 0-553-48228-9

Published simultaneously in the United States and Canada

Bantam Books are published by Bantam Books, a division of
Bantam Doubleday Dell Publishing Group, Inc. Its trademark,
consisting of the words "Bantam Books" and the portrayal of a
rooster, is registered in the U.S. Patent and Trademark Office
and in other countries. Marca Registrada. Bantam Books, 1540
Broadway, New York, New York 10036.

PRINTED IN THE UNITED STATES OF AMERICA

OPM   0 9 8 7 6 5 4

GRAVEYARD SCHOOL

Camp Dracula

CHAPTER
1

The blood-red sun was sinking fast over Camp Westerra.

Jeep dropped his duffel bag in the dirt. His father gunned the motor of the station wagon. The car disappeared in a cloud of dust, down the rutted road, into the shadowy trees.

Jeep wondered if he would ever see his parents again. His father was always getting lost.

That was why Jeep was so late to camp. The last one to arrive. Made to look weird from the beginning.

Not that he cared. He hated camp already. He didn't want to be there. All the other kids at Grove Hill Elementary School, also known as Graveyard School, got to have normal vacations as a reward for their school-year suffering. Or at least interesting ones.

But not me, thought Jeep.

He turned and looked the camp over. The buildings

looked as if they'd been made of Lincoln Logs. Fake. Phony. Unreal. Jeep eyed them suspiciously.

Just past the wooden split-rail fence surrounding the parking lot, a short path led to a log cabin with the words CAMP HEADQUARTERS carved into a rustic sign out front. Another sign on the front porch said INFIRMARY, with an arrow pointing around the side of the building. On the wall by the front door Jeep could see the outline of a map.

Beyond that was a bigger building, also made of logs, with a porch that went all the way around. He could barely make out the words MESS HALL on the sign in front of it.

And down the hill, surrounded by a dock and a diving tower and a row of canoes pulled up on the shore, was the lake. Lake Minaharker. He knew that from the camp flyers his mother had kept reading aloud to him.

Jeep hated getting wet.

It was almost dark now and he still didn't see any sign of life at the camp.

Great, thought Jeep. *My father probably got so lost that he drove me to the wrong camp. This one's probably abandoned because some ax murderer—*

"Hello."

Jeep spun around and tripped over his duffel bag. He made a grab for the gate and saved himself at the last minute.

"Owwww!" Jeep jerked his hand back. An enormous splinter was stuck in his thumb.

2

Trying to act cool, Jeep pulled the splinter out. He winced in spite of himself. The camp might look fake, but the pain was definitely real. A tiny, bright red bead of blood appeared on his thumb.

Jeep wiped his thumb on his jeans and looked up.

The tallest, thinnest, palest man Jeep had ever seen in his life stood there. The man was wearing a pith helmet, a black shirt with a red collar, baggy red shorts, and what looked like army boots. He had hair so blond, it was almost colorless. White-blond eyebrows showed above a pair of dark glasses.

Jeep could see the shrunken reflection of himself in the mirror of the dark glasses.

The glasses were focused on his hand. The one with the bloody thumb.

The man stuck out his own hand. He smiled at Jeep with thin red lips. His teeth were large and startlingly white.

"Welcome," said the man. "Welcome to Camp Westerra. I'm your camp director, Seward Renfield."

As Jeep stuck out his own hand, his injured thumb gave a nasty throb. "Oww!" said Jeep. At the last minute he pulled his hand back. He stuck his thumb in his mouth. "Sorry," Jeep mumbled. "Splinter in m'thumb."

Mr. Renfield stood there for a moment, his hand foolishly extended. Then he said, "I see." The dark glasses flashed—or maybe it was the eyes behind the dark glasses, the eyes that Jeep couldn't see.

"Ah," said Mr. Renfield. Then he said again, "I see."

He raised a clipboard he'd been holding in his other hand. "And you must be . . ."

"Jeep. Jeep Holmes." Jeep inspected his thumb. The bleeding had stopped.

"Yesss." The dark glasses focused once more on Jeep's injured hand. "Would you like to step around the corner of the house to our infirmary and have Nurse Hatchett take a look at that? We have a fully furnished wellness facility, and she's an excellent health care specialist. The health of our campers is *very* important to us."

"Er, no," said Jeep hastily. "No thanks."

Mr. Renfield paused. Then he said, "As you wish."

"So what's the drill?" asked Jeep.

The white eyebrows lifted on the pale white forehead. "Drill?" asked Mr. Renfield.

"You know. The story. What's happening? What am I supposed to do now?"

"Your enthusiasm indicates great Camp Westerra camper potential," said Mr. Renfield.

"I'm so excited," said Jeep sarcastically.

Mr. Renfield seemed to hear only what he wanted to hear. He ignored Jeep's sarcasm. He became very busy with his clipboard, flipping through sheets of paper. "Holmes," he murmured. "Holmes. Hmmm. Ah. Yes. You're a Bear. A Purple Bear."

"Purple Bear?" asked Jeep. "You're joking. Right?"

Again Mr. Renfield ignored Jeep.

"Our campers are divided into groups according to age and, of course, gender. Each group of campers is given

4

an animal name. There are eight groups, or outposts: four male and four female. In each outpost are four cabins.

"Each cabin is given a color. You are in the Bear Outpost. Your cabin is the purple cabin. Therefore you are a Purple Bear."

"At least I'm not a stupid purple dinosaur," Jeep muttered.

"Purple Bear," repeated the tall, pale camp director. "One of my favorites. An *especially* good cabin this summer."

Director Renfield reached into his hip pocket and pulled out a small booklet. He squinted at it, then handed it to Jeep. "Here you go, Jeep. Your very own map of the camp. It's a very simple map, as you see. The main activity cluster is right here around the shores of Lake Minaharker."

The director pointed to the sheet of dark water at the foot of the hill as if Jeep might not have noticed it before. "And that big house across the way there is the dining hall, or, as we like to call it, the mess hall. We have a small supply store there for stamps and so forth. The boys' cabins are back that way, behind my headquarters, and the girls' cabins are over that way, behind the mess hall. On the back of your map you'll find a list of the camp rules. Your counselor will go over everything with you and your new Purple Bear friends in a little while."

Jeep was barely able to keep himself from gagging.

Mr. Renfield went on smoothly, "Just take that trail

down there and follow the signs marked with the bear claw."

But Jeep had stopped listening. He was staring hard at a small, cavelike structure at one end of the porch. The opening to it was covered with wire mesh. "What's that?" he asked, pointing.

Mr. Renfield turned. "Bats," he said.

"Bats?" Jeep said. His voice went up into the sonar range. *"Bats?"*

"My pest-control patrol," said Renfield. "I let them out at night. They're quite effective at patrolling, er, controlling the pests. We have quite a mosquito population around the lake."

"I don't like bats," said Jeep flatly.

"An unfortunate prejudice," said Renfield. He seemed amused by Jeep's reaction. "But then, perhaps the bats don't like you, either. You'll be learning more about bats in our nature groups. As well as about other animals native to this region."

"I can hardly wait," Jeep said.

The path was soft and thickly coated in places with pine needles. The air smelled of pine trees and the lake. The last red spears of late-afternoon light pierced the dark woods.

It was very, very quiet.

Yep. No doubt about it. Camp Westerra had it all. Trees. Water. Fresh air.

Bats.

Jeep began to whistle.

He passed other wooden signs shaped like arrows pointing down other trails. Each arrow had a different symbol on it: an eagle, a deer, a raccoon. The trails were narrow and did not look particularly well used or well marked.

Jeep kept a sharp eye on the Bear Trail to make sure he didn't get lost. He hated the idea of getting lost in the woods even more than he hated the idea of bats.

He kept walking. He kept whistling. The trail went on and on.

He started to sweat.

The darkness was closing in fast. Without warning, the trail dipped steeply and divided. Jeep stopped and almost skidded out of control on the slippery pine needles. Then he saw the arrow with the bear-claw sign, pointing straight down at a crazy angle.

Great, thought Jeep. *My cabin's probably at the bottom of a mountain, about a hundred miles from the mess hall.* He shifted his backpack, tightened his grip on his duffel bag, and started forward.

If I was my father, I'd be lost by now, thought Jeep. *But I'm not. Not lost, that is.*

No, I'm not like my father, thought Jeep. *I have a map.*

He stopped and pulled out the map. He held it close to his nose and peered at it in the dying light of day.

"I'm *not* lost!" said Jeep aloud. He felt a little better. He folded the map up and started down the trail again. It didn't look as if he had very far to go.

Something rustled in the trees.

Jeep walked faster.

Something swooped out of the sky near his head.

In spite of himself Jeep ducked.

Whatever it was flickered away into the shadows, silent except for the faint sound of wings.

What kinds of sounds do bats make? Jeep wondered. He put the thought out of his mind, but he turned up the collar of his shirt. Just in case. He didn't like to think in case of what.

Another faint whoosh. Something black and swift passed him on one side.

He dodged it.

Then another streak from the darkness swooped near his head. Then another.

The faint whisper of wings grew louder and louder. It became a collection of whispers.

Jeep stopped. He forced himself to take a deep breath. Then looked up.

The sky was black with the crisscrossed flight of a hundred birds. There were so many that they were even blacker than the sky itself.

They didn't make a sound.

Then Jeep realized that they weren't birds at all.

They were bats.

Jeep ducked his head, and began to run for his life.

CHAPTER
2

The bats swooped out of the sky like a Halloween decoration gone mad. They swirled around him. Beneath tiny, alert ears, tiny wizened faces looked into his as they flicked past. Tiny humanoid mouths opened, showing needle-sharp teeth.

Jeep lashed out with his arms. Mysterious things brushed his hands, light as feathers.

Bat feathers?

Opening his mouth, Jeep tried to scream. But no sound would come out.

He was doomed. He was batfood.

He was in such a panic that he didn't hear the crashing in the woods nearby.

All he could hear was the rasp of his breath.

He never saw what hit him.

"Ugh!" grunted Jeep.
"Hey. Owww. Watch it!" someone complained.

A boy about Jeep's height, but almost as wide as he was tall, recoiled from Jeep. Jeep pitched forward onto the pine needles and rolled, letting go of his duffel bag and covering his head with his hands.

He found his voice at last. "Get them off, get them off!" he shrieked. "Get them off me!"

Something touched his arm.

He kicked at it.

"Oww!" said the voice again. "What are you doing? Are you crazy?"

Slowly Jeep lowered his arms.

"Are you okay?" said the boy standing on the trail above him.

"Wh-What?"

"Are you okay?" a voice repeated.

Jeep sat up.

The boy was bending over to inspect Jeep now. "Are you hurt?" he asked.

Even in the early-evening gloom Jeep could see that the kid looked as if he'd just stepped out of a store. All his clothes looked painfully clean—or painfully new. His jeans were stiff and sharply creased. His red shirt was bright and unfaded. His white sneakers practically glowed in the dark.

"Who are you?" croaked Jeep.

"Martin," said the boy. He pushed back the red cap he was wearing, then stuck out his hand. For a moment Jeep thought the boy was trying to shake hands. Then he realized that the kid was offering to help him up.

He grabbed the kid's hand and rose to his feet. The kid looked like he was clumsy, but Jeep had to admit that he was surprisingly strong.

"Thanks," said Jeep. His voice still sounded like a frog's. He cleared his throat. His heartbeat began to return to normal. "Thanks," he said again.

"No problem," said the kid. "Sorry I scared you."

"You didn't scare me," said Jeep. "They did."

Martin looked up in the direction Jeep was pointing. Something dark wheeled away between the trees. Otherwise it was still.

"What did?"

"The bats!" Jeep practically yelled. "The bats! Thousands of them. There's one now!"

Martin looked puzzled. Then he set down his backpack, unzipped it, reached inside, and pulled out a pair of binoculars. He lifted the binoculars to his eyes and focused overhead. "A common fruit bat," he announced. "Quite an intelligent mammal. Nothing to be afraid of, really."

Jeep eyed him curiously. "Are you related to Renfield or something? Or to any of his little pet bats?"

"Related to Mr. Renfield? No," said Martin, laughing. "But I'm familiar with his bats. He doesn't have *thousands* of them. . . . Are you sure you weren't, you know, imagining things?"

"No! I mean, yes, I'm sure. I know what I saw! They attacked me. Hundreds and thousands of bats."

Martin frowned. "They *attacked* you? Are you sure?"

Jeep couldn't believe it. "Are you blind or something!" he shouted.

Ducking his head, Martin said, "No. Well, not exactly." He pointed to his eyes. "Contacts. I just got them. My father made me. I keep losing my glasses. Mostly I step on them or something when I'm not wearing them because I can't see."

"I don't believe this," said Jeep. "I don't believe it." He began looking around for his duffel bag.

"It's the reason I didn't see you until you ran into me." Martin smiled apologetically. "I got something in my eye. Between that and my contact lenses I kinda, you know, couldn't see. My glasses are in my suitcase, and I—"

"Why me?" Jeep moaned. He spotted his duffel bag. He pushed past Martin and went to pick it up. "You didn't see a huge, enormous flock of bats swoop down out of the sky and try to kill me?"

"No!" said Martin. "That could never happen! Bats don't behave that way! You can't believe everything you see in old Alfred Hitchcock movies, you know."

Jeep looked up. Not a bat in sight. Just the darkening sky and the branches of trees.

Martin changed the subject, asking soothingly, "This is your first time at Camp Westerra, right?"

"Yep," said Jeep.

"You ever been to camp before?"

"Nope."

"Well, camp—nature—sometimes takes some getting used to."

"I know a bat when I see a bat," said Jeep, growing annoyed. "And I can count. To about a thousand bats. Which is what I saw." He paused, checking the trail sign, and turned. "Nice meeting you, Martin."

"Wait!" cried Martin. "I didn't mean . . . well, wait. Where are you going?"

Jeep stopped and sighed. "To my cabin," he said impatiently.

"Hey," Martin said eagerly. "I'll walk with you. Just let me get my suitcase."

"Suitcase?" said Jeep.

Martin stumbled back up the trail and plunged out of sight into the trees. A moment later he emerged, dragging an enormous old red suitcase. Jeep smirked, noticing that the suitcase matched Martin's cap. And his shirt. Martin looked like an advertisement for *Nerds at Camp.*

Jeep groaned inwardly. He couldn't believe he'd ended up with this geek. But what could he do? He turned and started down the trail.

"You're in Bear, too," said Martin as if he'd discovered something amazing. "Or you wouldn't be on the Bear Trail, right? Bear's a good group. I've never gotten to be in Bear before. What color is your cabin?"

"Purple," Jeep mumbled.

"Purple? Really?" Martin looked genuinely delighted. "That's great!"

Jeep didn't answer. He was brooding.

Although he didn't like to admit it, he was worried. Camp had gotten off to a very bad start.

• • •

"Here we are!" said Martin.

Jeep stopped. The path had ended. A sign to one side of it read BEAR OUTPOST. Beyond the sign was a clearing surrounded by five small cabins.

Outlines of bears in red, green, yellow, and purple were painted on signs above the doors of four of the cabins. Above the door of the fifth cabin was a sign with a bigger, brown bear on it. The words on the sign said LEADER BEAR.

At the far end of the clearing was a sign that said BATHHOUSE, with an arrow pointing down a short trail to another small building that stood partly hidden the woods.

"Isn't this great?" said Martin. He pointed. "There's Purple Bear, right there at the end of the row. C'mon!"

Martin charged enthusiastically forward.

Jeep followed more slowly.

Trailing Martin, Jeep walked up the three steps to the front door of Purple Bear and pushed it open. He was instantly greeted by a guy with bleached-blond hair and big white teeth. "Hello!" the guy cried, bounding forward.

Jeep stopped. He frowned. "Hello," he replied.

Two other campers had claimed the bunks against either wall at the far end of the room. They were unpacking, but they stopped to stare at Jeep.

"This is Jeep," Martin said. "Jeep, this is Lucian Noir and William Ang."

Since Jeep couldn't stare back at both of them at the same time, he decided to ignore them.

"Hello there, Jeep!" the blond guy continued. "I'm your Bear Leader. Welcome to Purple Bear."

"Gee, thanks," said Jeep.

"My name is Peter, but you can call me Pete," the counselor went on. He had an obnoxious tan, Jeep noted, which must have extended from his hairline to his hiking boots. It looked fake.

"So where do I put my stuff, Pete?" Jeep asked, trying to get rid of him.

"It's Jeep's first time at Camp Westerra," explained Martin.

"Ah," Pete said. Giving Jeep a big wink, he waved his hand at William, Lucian, and Martin. "First come, first choice on bunks here at Camp Westerra, Jeep. The sun never sets on fun, but we never forget that the early bird gets the worm. Looks like your bunkmates have beat you to the best bunkaroos. Ha, ha!"

"Thanks," said Jeep. "But I don't like worms anyway."

Pete's smile faded. He looked puzzled for a moment. Then his face lit up and his smile returned. "A joke! Ha, ha, ha! I like a camper with a sense of humor."

This is pathetic, Jeep thought. Ignoring Pete, Jeep continued checking out the cabin. It was small. Low cots were pushed into each corner of the cabin. Closets were built against the walls between the bunk beds. Above each bunk bed on either side of the closets were screened windows. The walls were rough, unfinished logs and the floors were wide, smooth wooden planks.

Jeep dumped his duffel back on the empty bunk behind the open door of the cabin.

Pete laughed heartily. "Okay, Bear campers. Get settled in and get acquainted. Make new friends, but keep the old. Almost time for dinner. See you later. I have to make the rounds, you know. The Bear Leader's work is never done!"

Then Pete leaped through the door and was gone.

"Is he weird, or what?" asked Jeep as soon as Pete was out of hearing.

No one answered. Jeep looked up to find Lucian, William, and Martin staring at him. Lucian had short red hair and dark brown eyes. Like Pete, Lucian was wearing khaki shorts with dozens of pockets, a short-sleeved blue cotton shirt with some kind of animal insignia above the left pocket, and hiking boots with thick socks that matched his shirt. William, who had dark brown hair and dark brown eyes, was wearing almost exactly the same thing except that his shirt was mustard yellow and his socks were white.

"Is there a dress code or something?" Jeep joked.

No one laughed. William and Lucian kept staring at Jeep. Martin stared down at his feet.

Jeep grew annoyed. "Why don't you guys take a picture? It lasts longer."

Lucian suddenly burst out laughing. "Good one," he said. "Good one, Jeep!"

"It wasn't that funny," said Jeep.

"It *was*," insisted Lucian.

"No it wasn't!" said William. He folded his arms and glared at Lucian.

At last Lucian stopped laughing. He gave Jeep a friendly grin. "You've never been to camp before?" he asked.

"No," said Jeep. "Up until this summer I was lucky."

William scowled harder. Martin looked worried. But Lucian just smiled. "Sheets and blankets are in your closet," Lucian volunteered, pointing. "Westerra's not like other camps, you know. It's pretty cool. We—"

"If he can't take it, he can go home," William interrupted.

"Thanks," said Jeep to Lucian. "Do we have to keep our beds made and stuff like that? What're the rules?"

"The rules?" said Lucian. "Oh, you know, you have to eat what you kill and—"

"We're going *hunting?*" Jeep said.

But even as he finished asking, he realized he'd fallen for Lucian's dumb joke.

Martin said quickly, "No. You don't have to make your bed, you can just pull your blanket up over everything. You can stow stuff under it, too. You just can't trash the cabin or anything."

"Thanks, Martin," said Jeep. He finished unpacking without saying anything else. When he'd gotten his bunk more or less made up, he sat down and looked around the cabin again.

Lucian, who was sitting on his own bunk watching Jeep, smiled harder .

Martin began to arrange his shirts in his closet by color.

William stretched his own blanket even more tightly across his own bunk and smoothed out an invisible wrinkle.

"So I saw these bats when I was coming down the, uh, Bear Trail," said Jeep casually. Jeep was aware of Martin's quick look. But Martin didn't say anything.

"What's the matter? Did they scare you?" asked William, sneering slightly.

"No," said Jeep. He narrowed his eyes at Martin, daring him to speak.

Martin didn't.

"Bats are kind of the camp mascot," said Lucian. "Mr. Renfield, our camp director—"

"I know. I met him. And his bats," said Jeep. He didn't add that the bats had nearly killed him.

Suddenly the screen door flew open and hit Jeep in the knee. He barely managed to stifle a yelp as Pete bounded back into the cabin. Pete crossed the room, took a quarter out of his pocket, and threw it down, edge first, on William's neatly made bed.

Jeep's eyes widened. The quarter had actually *bounced*. William had his blanket and sheets stretched so tightly across his bed that the quarter had bounced up like a ball.

Catching the quarter in the air, Pete stuffed it back in his pocket. "Well done, William, well done!" He chuckled and turned to the others. "Now, here's a camper who knows how to set a good example."

Clang! Boing! Clang!

"There it is!" said Pete. "Get a move on, guys! Time to say 'Helloooo, Campers.' Time to head up to Camp Central to meet 'n' greet! We'll gather in front of Leader Bear in five minutes."

Jeep shook his head. Hello, campers? Camp Central? Leader Bear?

William and Lucian sprinted out of the cabin after Pete.

Martin hovered in the doorway, a worried look on his face. "Jeep? Aren't you coming? Jeep?"

Jeep groaned. He stood up and walked slowly out of the cabin with Martin.

It was nearly dark. Jeep hated to admit it, but he was glad he was walking in the middle of a group of people. He hated camp. And he was pretty sure he hated most of the campers.

But he figured that as long as he was in the middle of a crowd, he was safe from whatever was out there in those woods.

CHAPTER

3

"Dip and pullll, dip and pullll." The counselor's dark glasses glinted in the morning sun. The water from Lake Minaharker glistened on the paddles of the canoe.

Martin dipped his paddle in the water and gave a mighty pull. The canoe swerved sideways.

Jeep, who was sitting in the canoe behind Martin, said, "Hey, watch ou—"

The canoe crashed into another canoe with a horrible grinding sound. The two girls in the canoe began to laugh. Martin turned bright red beneath his red baseball hat. "Sorry," he mumbled.

The girl who was steering suddenly stopped her odd cackling. "Don't worry," she said. "These are just aluminum canoes. It's not like they're real ones or anything. Or like those cool guide boats they have up in the Adirondacks. Those are made of wood and they c thousands—"

"Dawn, please," said the dark-haired girl in the front of the canoe. "Like we care."

Dawn shot the girl a disgusted look and flipped her own red-brown braid over her shoulder, but she stopped talking. She dipped her paddle in the water, and the canoe shot forward across the lake.

"Excellent, excellent," called the canoe instructor, a skinny girl who looked as if she hadn't been fed in weeks. Martin lifted his paddle to try again just as Jeep said quickly, "Let's just rest for a moment. We've been working pretty hard."

Martin didn't argue. He laid his paddle across his sunburned knees. Although they'd only been at camp one day, Martin had already managed to get lost going from Purple Bear to the mess hall, get whacked in the forehead by a branch, spill orange juice all over his shirt at the breakfast table, *and* get totally sunburned despite the fact that he spent half his time slathering himself with super sunblock.

"This is the first time I haven't turned a canoe over during a lesson," said Martin happily.

Jeep didn't want to point out that the lesson wasn't over yet. So he didn't say anything.

All around them the campers paddled and splashed and shouted on the dark waters of Lake Minaharker. Jeep didn't like the lake. It was cold and dark. Jeep hated cold water, and he really hated water where he couldn't see the bottom. He was a good swimmer and he knew it was silly, but he couldn't convince himself that something he couldn't see wasn't just waiting in the murky depths to pull him under. He never, ever went swimming in the lake near his home in Grove Hill. Everyone called that lake Slime Lake. His friends, were all probably hanging out there right now. Even though Jeep wouldn't swim in Slime Lake, he'd give anything to be there, too. . . .

Lake Minaharker looked plain *evil*. It was a dark, muddy red color that made the bottom of the lake impossible to see, even in the shallow water around the edge.

The sun was beating down hotter than ever. Martin took his sunblock out of his shorts pocket and began to slather it on. Jeep stared out across the lake. In the far corner of the canoe area Dawn and the dark-haired girl were gliding swiftly over the water, cutting neatly in and out among the other canoes.

The other canoers didn't seem to notice the heat and the sun. They paddled on and on like obedient campers. Many of them were as sunburned as Martin. Some of them looked even worse. Almost all of them wore the same kind of multipocketed shorts that William, Lucian, and Pete had been wearing on the first day of camp and that Martin had switched into. Martin's were a funny green color. With his sunburned knees and red cap, they made him look like a Christmas-tree ornament.

They should call this place Camp Sunburn, thought Jeep. They might be super campers, but about half the campers with light skin were frying like eggs—and the campers with darker skin didn't look too happy, either. It made Jeep feel better. He wasn't any nature boy, but at least he wasn't a fry-baby.

The canoe instructor, a counselor named Elizabetta, blasted on her whistle. "Everybody to the shore," she called.

Jeep wasn't sure what happened next. One minute he was dipping his paddle in the water, slowly turning the nose of the canoe toward the half-moon of shoreline where the canoes were docked, and the next minute the whole canoe was tilting wildly.

As the world swung in a crazy arc before his eyes, Jeep saw Martin struggling to his knees, his paddle waving wildly.

"Sit!" shrieked Jeep. "Sit still, Martin!"

Martin turned around. The canoe tipped. Jeep saw Martin's mouth open, but he never heard what Martin was going to say. The canoe flipped completely over, and Jeep's eyes, nose, mouth, and ears filled with the dark, cold water of Lake Minaharker.

He opened his eyes. He couldn't see a thing. The water was as dark as it looked from above. Something hit him in the stomach.

He punched out. A hand grabbed his arm and pulled him down.

He punched out again and felt his own hand hit something soft and yielding. The hand let go.

Another hand caught the back of his shirt and pulled

him up out of the water. "Put your feet down!" a voice shouted in his ear.

He put his feet down and they touched rocky lake bottom. He stood up and realized he was chest deep in the water.

Dawn and her friend were in the canoe next to him. His canoe was floating on its side just out of Jeep's reach. Martin was still thrashing wildly nearby.

With a quick stroke of her paddle Dawn pulled her canoe up beside Martin. She leaned over and shouted, "Hey! You can stand up! Hey!"

Jeep started to warn Dawn not to get too close to Martin. But he was too late. Martin reached out and grabbed Dawn. Dawn's canoe rocked wildly. The dark-haired girl said, "Stop it!" and quickly leaned against the angle the canoe was tilting. She began to backpaddle at the same time. She kept the canoe from turning over. But she wasn't able to save Dawn.

With a splash and a shriek of rage, Dawn was pulled into the lake, too.

A moment later, sputtering and angry, Dawn fought free of Martin and stood up. She punched Martin hard, not being careful about where she hit him.

"Owww!" choked Martin.

"Stand up, you nerd!" ordered Dawn. *"Stand up."*

This time Martin heard her. He put his feet down. He stood up. The water came only to his waist.

Jeep snagged the canoe paddle that was floating nearby.

"You are *such* a klutz!" Dawn shrieked. "You ought to know by now that the lake isn't deep here! Don't you turn your canoe over all the time? Don't you learn *anything*?"

"I'm sorry," said Martin sheepishly. "Good thing I wasn't wearing my contacts, huh? They could have been washed right out of my eyes."

"Wow, I was *worried*," Jeep said, exasperated.

Martin took off his glasses and tried unsuccessfully to wipe the water off them with the end of his wet shirt. Canoers glided past the wet threesome on either side, snickering and offering sarcastic advice.

"Okay, campers, the show is over. Let's finish beaching our canoes," Elizabetta said briskly.

"I'll dock our canoe, Dawn," Dawn's canoe partner volunteered, still keeping the canoe at a safe distance from Martin.

"Gee, thanks, Nora," Dawn said sarcastically. She turned her back on Nora and waded out to Jeep and Martin's overturned canoe. She flipped it upright with one deft move and began to pull it toward shore.

Jeep grabbed the other paddle and followed her.

"I'm sorry," said Martin helplessly. He put his glasses back on and began to wade after them.

By the time they reached the shore, the other campers had finished putting their canoes on the canoe racks. They stood and watched silently as Dawn and Jeep carried the last canoe over and settled it in place. No one offered to help. They just stood there, staring at Jeep and Dawn and Martin. It was like being on a stage. It was unnerving.

Then Jeep noticed a tall, thin, motionless figure in a pith helmet standing next to the canoe instructor. It was Mr. Renfield.

"A little accident?" asked Mr. Renfield in his cold, flat voice.

"Sort of," said Jeep.

"You seem to be accident-prone," said Mr. Renfield. He smiled a thin-lipped smile.

"What are you talking about?" asked Jeep. *How does the director know about those bats?* he wondered.

But before he could give himself away, the director went on, "You fell and got that nasty splinter in your thumb, now you fall out of the canoe. . . . No . . . cuts, or anything of that nature?" The director looked almost hungrily at Jeep.

In spite of himself Jeep took a step back. "No."

The canoe instructor said, "Everybody just got a little wet, Mr. Renfield. . . . Okay, time to go to your next activities, campers. Dawn, you and Martin and Jeep need to go get into some dry clothes. If you'll tell me your schedules, I'll let your counselors for your next activities know you'll be a little late."

Jeep barely listened as he watched the silent audience of campers turn away. It was as if they couldn't take their eyes off him. As if he were some kind of freak.

And the camp director was even worse. Where did he get the right to make him sound like some kind of world-class klutz? So Jeep wasn't the greatest camper in the world. So what? It wasn't like they hadn't seen Martin turn a canoe over year after year. Jeep didn't get it. It gave him the creeps.

It made him angry.

"Run along, now," said Elizabetta. She patted Jeep on the shoulder.

Jeep looked up. "Oh. Yeah. Right."

"Thanks!" said Martin brightly.

Both Jeep and Dawn gave him dirty looks. Then they started up the hill toward the trails to the cabins.

"I don't believe this," said Dawn. "In all the years I've been a camper, I've never, ever turned over a canoe. Thanks, you big, stupid—"

"Knock it off," said Jeep.

"You might say thank you," Dawn said, putting her hands on her hips. "I could have just stood there and watched you drown yourself in two feet of water."

"I would have figured it out," said Jeep angrily.

"Yeah, right," said Dawn. She rolled her eyes.

"At least you didn't turn your canoe over, Dawn," said Martin. "You just fell in the water."

"Just . . . fell . . . in . . . the . . . water." Dawn glared at Martin. "You don't get it, do you? I didn't even want to come to this stupid camp this year!"

"Hey! Me either," said Jeep, forgetting that he'd just about decided that Dawn was the most obnoxious girl on the face of the planet. "I mean, who ever heard of this place? And you've got to admit, it is strange. Really strange."

"Strange?" Dawn turned her attention to Jeep. "Strange? What's strange is what a bunch of babies everybody is. Afraid of a little sunburn. Afraid of their own shadows! It's a big camp for big babies. I mean, puhlease. Planned activities. Swimming. Arts and crafts? Making little plaster-of-paris casts of animal footprints? Campfire stories? Give me a break!"

"Hey, I agree," said Jeep.

That stopped Dawn. "You do?"

"Totally. I mean, I'd much rather be someplace else."

"You don't mean that!" Martin said, shocked.

Ignoring Martin, Dawn said to Jeep, "I wanted to go to Outward Bound. Or hike one of those mountains in the Adirondacks in New York that don't have trails. You know, one of the really tall mountains. The kind people get lost on and fall off of and die." She paused a moment, her eyes glowing at the thought. Then she said, "So, what did you want to do?"

Jeep shrugged. "A friend of mine, Skip, went with his family on a wolf-watching expedition to Alaska. That would have been cool. Or I could have gone to baseball camp like another guy at my school, Park. Or maybe I just would have gone to the beach."

"The beach?" said Dawn, as if Jeep were using words she didn't understand.

"The beach," said Jeep. "Sand. Sun. Surf."

"Sharks," said Dawn, becoming enthusiastic again.

"No sharks," said Jeep. "I don't do sharks."

"Oh." Dawn looked at Jeep. "I didn't think you were a *real* camper," she said.

She turned and walked away before Jeep could answer.

"Oh yeah?" Jeep sputtered. "Oh yeah?" Then he shouted after her, "Oh yeah? Well, I'm glad I'm not a real camper! I wouldn't want to be like the other campers around here for anything!"

Dawn stopped. She turned. She studied Jeep for a moment. "Well," she said at last, "at least you're honest."

She turned back down the trail. "See ya later," she said over her shoulder in the friendliest tone Jeep had heard her use.

"What a weirdo," said Jeep.

"Yeah," said Martin.

Jeep looked at Martin out of the corner of his eye. But Martin didn't seem to see anything ironic in calling another person weird.

That's the trouble with weirdos, thought Jeep. *They never know they're weirdos.*

Suddenly Jeep began to worry that he was turning into a weirdo, too. Was that what Camp Westerra was doing to him? After only a couple of days?

Jeep didn't want to think about it. He turned abruptly and headed toward the Bear Outpost. Martin ambled along behind him. Martin's sneakers made disgusting sucking, squishing noises with every step he took. So did Jeep's. He looked down at his feet.

His dirty old white sneakers had been stained bright red by the lake water.

"Ugh," said Jeep.

Jeep thought of the bats. He thought of falling into the dark lake.

Better weird than dead, thought Jeep. Or did he mean that the other way around?

CHAPTER

4

"**Camp Wes...ter...ra** forevv...er...brave ...annn...d...true."

The campers stopped singing and stood in a semicircle around the flagpole at the center of the camp. Slowly, reverently, the flag guard from Green Eagle lowered the camp flag and began to fold it up for the night.

Lucian hadn't been kidding about a bat being the camp mascot. The big red camp flag had a silhouette of a black bat right in the center, above the words CAMP WESTERRA embroidered in black Gothic lettering.

"We might get to do that one night," Martin whispered to Jeep.

"Why?" said Jeep. He meant, why would anyone want to? He had no interest in being a flag guard for Camp Westerra.

But Martin misunderstood. "Because campers from every group are chosen, two different campers each night, to be the flag guard. It's a real honor."

Somehow Jeep knew without asking that Martin had never been chosen to be a flag guard. Martin had probably never been chosen to be anything, thought Jeep, except last.

And now Martin had become his friend. Martin, a book-reading klutz whom Jeep wouldn't have even gone near back home in Grove Hill.

But not at Camp Westerra. At Camp Westerra Jeep was a misfit for the first time in his life. Even more of a misfit than Martin, who at least *loved* camp and wanted to be a good camper.

All Jeep wanted was to be gone.

The camp director blew his whistle for attention as the flag was carried to the closet in the camp headquarters where it was stored.

"Okay, campers," boomed the director. "Let's lay some trail back to our cabins. You're going to get a surprise tonight."

"Wowwww," said Martin. "A surprise."

"I can hardly wait," said Jeep, bored.

Across the circle he saw Dawn. She looked about as enthusiastic as Jeep felt. Less so, in fact. When Mr. Renfield made the announcement about the surprise, she yawned. It was such a big yawn, Jeep could practically see her tonsils. She didn't even try to hide it. Some of the girls around Dawn looked shocked. Some giggled.

Dawn was a misfit, too. But Jeep suspected that she enjoyed it.

As they hiked back to their cabins in the late-afternoon shadows, Jeep stopped. He looked over his shoulder at Martin.

Martin was even more sunburned now. Even his eyes looked sunburned. They were practically glowing in the dark.

"Shhh! What was that noise?" Jeep asked.

"What noise?" asked Martin. He laughed. "The bats won't hurt you, Jeep. Really."

"Never mind," said Jeep, annoyed.

Ahead he heard the crash of the other campers as they turned off in groups onto the trails that led to their outposts. Almost everybody had passed Jeep and Martin as they trudged along.

Like they hadn't spent a whole day canoeing and swimming and wearing themselves out with nature activities. Like the setting sun marked the beginning instead of the end of the day.

"What do you think the surprise is?" asked Martin. He grinned. "I bet I know."

Jeep didn't answer. He was sure he'd heard a sound in the woods behind them.

"There's no one behind us, is there, Martin?"

Martin turned and flicked his flashlight up the trail. "Nope. We're the last ones."

Jeep stared hard into the darkness.

But he couldn't see anything at all.

He was losing his mind, that's what it was. No, he was

tired. That was it. Tired. That was why he felt as if something was watching him. As if something was slinking along in the underbrush nearby . . . stalking him. Thinking about having him for dinner. . . .

It had been a long day. A long, long day.

And it wasn't over yet.

"I knew it," Martin exclaimed as they came into the Bear group clearing.

Pete was standing in the middle of the clearing, motioning them forward. He was holding a flashlight under his chin with one hand so that his face looked ghastly and strange. He was making weird moaning sounds.

"Ghost stories! We're going to tell ghost stories," said Martin.

That's all I need, thought Jeep. But he said to Martin, "Just great."

"And then there came a knocking on the cabin door. . . . Knock. Knock. Knock. And a voice from the other side said, 'Who's got my head? I want my head back. . . . ' "

"Tame," said Jeep. "Very tame. Where I come from, we have a headless ghost that could take this ghost *out.*"

"Really?" Martin breathed. He turned his head, and the firelight flickered on his glasses, hiding his eyes. "Cool."

Jeep shifted restlessly as Pete went on, the flashlight still trained beneath his chin. He yawned. He looked around the circle of faces. Many of the other campers had their flashlights switched on and were resting their chins on them, too.

It had a nice, creepy effect.

But childish, thought Jeep.

Beside him Martin leaned forward again to listen to Pete, letting his mouth drop slightly open.

Jeep swallowed another yawn. He unfolded his legs and folded them again. Finally he leaned over and whispered in Martin's sunburned ear, "I'm going to the bathroom."

"Uh-huh," said Martin, nodding slightly, still staring at Pete.

Jeep got up and edged away from the circle of campers around Pete. Pete's voice droned on and on behind him as he walked past the cabins to the trail to the bathroom. Insects swarmed around a dim light above the bathroom door.

Something bit Jeep on the side of the neck. He slapped at it and looked at his hand. The bloody smear of a mosquito was spread across his fingers.

Jeep made a face and wiped his hands on his jeans. He'd forgotten to put on his repellant. *Where are the mosquito-eating bats now?* he thought.

The door of the bathhouse slammed open so suddenly that Jeep jumped back. A tall, thin figure was silhouetted in the doorway.

For one awful moment Jeep thought it was Renfield. Then he realized it was Lucian. "Hey, watch it," Jeep snapped.

"Did I . . . scare you?" asked Lucian.

"No," said Jeep. "But you might have."

"Oh. Sorry," said Lucian. He smiled. He didn't sound sorry at all.

Jeep went into the bathhouse. Unlike the cabins, it wasn't made of wood but of cement. It was cold and clammy and pretty primitive. The showers were at one end. The toilet stalls were at the other. The sinks were in the middle at the back.

"Hello?" called Jeep as he stepped inside the door.

No one answered. He looked around. In spite of himself he went over to the showers and peered inside each one of them.

No one was there. No one was in any of the bathroom stalls, either. He pushed open every door until he came to the one at the end, just to make sure.

He turned around.

The crickets and tree frogs were making an awful racket outside. Insects bombed against the screen door.

Other than that he was alone.

He felt pretty silly. What did he think was going to happen? Did he really believe that something was going to come swimming up out of the pipes from Lake Mina-harker and get him?

"Grow up," he muttered to himself.

Jeep pushed open a stall door. He stepped inside.

He heard a faint, whispering sound.

And then the lights went out.

"Hey!" said Jeep.

Something scuttled across the floor from the direction of the door. He heard it coming. Coming toward him. He turned and crashed into the side of the stall.

Something touched his ankle.

Jeep gave a strangled cry and kicked out. His foot hit the toilet. Hard.

He let out a howl.

He hopped back and fell against the stall door, and it flew open. Jeep flopped out onto his back on the cold, clammy cement floor. For a moment he couldn't breathe.

Then he heard the scrabbling again.

Jeep rolled over and jumped up and ran blindly toward where he thought the door was.

Something swooped down. He couldn't get away. He was trapped.

He fought with all his might. His feet slipped out from under him. His hand hit something knobby and hard.

He fell heavily to the floor of the shower, tangled up in the shower curtain as the shower knob he'd hit released a spray of freezing water.

And the lights in the bathhouse came back on.

Jeep didn't know how long he sat there in the cold shower, trying to gather his scattered wits. He'd started to shiver before he got slowly to his feet and turned off the water. He flung the mutilated shower curtain down in the shower. He stepped cautiously out of the shower stall.

No one was there. No one. Nothing.

No small animal on whispery, scrabbly, clawlike feet.

Jeep decided he wasn't going to wait around for the lights to go out again. He dashed across the bathhouse and pushed open the screen door, listening to his feet make wet, slurpy, skidding sounds. No one had missed him. The Bears were still gathered around the campfire telling stupid ghost stories.

But Jeep had had enough for one day. For the second time he went back to his cabin and changed out of his wet clothes. This time he got into bed. He was tired. He needed to rest.

And at least in his cabin nothing could happen to him. Just in case, though, he put his flashlight under his pillow. He wasn't taking any chances of getting caught in the dark ever again.

Then he pulled the covers over his head. And to make doubly sure he was safe, he stayed awake until William, Lucian, and Martin had returned from the campfire.

He didn't know what woke him.

The cabin was very dark. Martin was snoring softly in the bunk across the way. William and Lucian were sleeping quietly in their own bunks. As his eyes adjusted to the darkness, he could see the slightly darker outline of their shapes on their beds.

He heard an owl hoot, then stop abruptly.

He reached out and let his fingers close around the reassuring weight of his flashlight.

And then he heard it. A whispering, scrabbling sound on the floor near the other end of the cabin.

His fingers tightened on the flashlight.

What was it?

Was something following him?

But what? And why?

Again. Scrabbling. Whispering. The skitter of claws over the wooden floor.

It was coming toward him. He held his breath and listened to it come closer. Closer. Closer.

And then it stopped.

Jeep broke out in a sweat. Where was it? What was it? What was it doing?

And then he knew. He felt it. A faint tug on the blankets. . . .

Jeep raised his flashlight and clicked it on just as the thing climbed up over the foot of his bed.

CHAPTER
5

"AAAAAAAAAAAAAAAHhhhhhh!"

It had long, long white teeth. Bloody red eyes. For a moment it seemed to fill up the whole room. It seemed to tower over him, ready to swoop down.

Jeep threw his flashlight.

Martin shouted, "What is it?"

"AAAArrrraaaaaaaahhhhhaaaa . . . rratt. A rat. It's a rat!" Jeep screamed. He couldn't control his voice.

He sounded like a teakettle.

The rat vanished.

William's voice said crossly, "Who's screaming?"

Then the door to the cabin slammed open and a dim lightbulb went on. Pete stood beneath it. He let go of the light-switch chain and began to fumble with the sash of his faded red bathrobe. His hair was sticking out. He had a hiking boot on one foot and a sneaker on the other.

He didn't look happy. "What's going on here?" he demanded.

"Jeep had a bad dream," said Martin quickly.

"It wasn't a dream! I know what I saw!" Jeep heard his voice go into teakettle-whistle range again and stopped. He tried to speak calmly. "I . . . woke up and this humongous, enormous, gigantic rat was sitting on the end of my bed. Staring at me. I threw my flashlight at it, and it ran away toward Lucian's bed."

Everyone looked over at Lucian.

He was still asleep, his body a hump beneath the blanket.

"Lucian," said Pete sharply.

Lucian didn't answer. Pete crossed the cabin to Lucian's bed and bent over and put his hands on Lucian's shoulder. "Lucian, wake up."

"It was a dream," Martin whispered softly, almost to himself.

The rat killed him, thought Jeep wildly. He looked over at Martin and saw the horrified expression on Martin's face as Martin stared at Lucian's motionless form.

Martin believes me, thought Jeep. *Why does he keep saying it's a dream?*

"Lucian, wake up!" Pete ordered.

Slowly Lucian moved. He sat up. He yawned. He looked around the cabin. He looked up at Pete, then looked quickly away. "I was asleep," he said. "Why'dja wake me up?"

"Jeep thought he saw a rat in the cabin," said Pete. "It ran in your direction."

"A rat?" Lucian's sleepy eyes widened. "Cool. Where is it?" He looked around.

Pete took a flashlight from the pocket of his bathrobe. He inspected the corners of the cabin. He looked in the closets. He looked under the beds. He checked the tightly fastened window screens. He shined the flashlight up at the roof and over the rafters of the cabin.

"Nothing," he reported at last, switching off his flashlight. "No rat. I don't see how a rat could have gotten in. A mouse maybe. Whatever, it's gone."

"If there ever *was* anything," said William. "Good one, Jeep. Way to go. Big ha ha." William flopped back into bed and pulled his blanket up. "I'm tired."

"It's late," said Pete. "You boys need to get some sleep. Jeep—you gonna be okay?"

Jeep looked at his cabin mates. William looked sleepy and grouchy. Lucian yawned, but he was watching Jeep with bright eyes. Martin, who hadn't put on his glasses, was squinting in Jeep's direction with a worried expression on his face.

What could Jeep say? "I'm fine," he said. "Probably was a dream."

Pete smiled in relief. "Those ghost stories'll getcha every time," he said. He yanked the overhead light chain, and the cabin went dark. A moment later the cabin door slammed shut behind him.

"You're not scared, are you, Jeep?" Martin whispered in the darkness.

"Shut up, Martin," said William. "I want to go to sleep."

"He's not scared," said Lucian softly. A sudden beam of light blinded Jeep. Lucian had his flashlight pointed directly in Jeep's face.

Jeep put his hand in front of his eyes. "Hey! Why are you trying to blind me?"

"Jeep's not afraid of a rat. Are you, Jeep?" Lucian kept the light in Jeep's eyes.

"Depends on the rat," said Jeep. He was getting annoyed. "Turn off the light. And the questions. Okay?"

Lucian laughed. He turned off his flashlight. Spots danced in front of Jeep's eyes.

"Hooray for Jeep. He's not afraid of the big, bad rat," said William sarcastically. "Now, could we go to sleep, please?"

"Fine by me," said Jeep. He flopped back on the bed and pulled the covers up.

Everyone fell silent.

Jeep listened to the silence. He listened to the crickets. He listened to the wind in the limbs of the trees. He listened as William began to snore loudly, like a cartoon character.

He listened to Lucian tossing and turning. Then Lucian began to breathe slowly and deeply.

Jeep turned on his side. He propped himself up on his elbow. "Martin," he whispered as loudly as he dared.

William kept snoring. Lucian slept on.

"Martin!"

Martin said, so softly that Jeep barely heard him, "Shhh! . . . What?"

"You believe me, don't you? You know it's true. You know I saw that giant mutant rat."

Lucian rolled over and muttered in his sleep.

A long silence followed.

Then Martin whispered, "Yes."

"Why'd you pretend you didn't believe me? Why'd you lie?"

"Shhh," hissed Martin.

"What's going on, Martin? What is it I'm not getting about camp? Is it some kind of joke? Some kind of initiation?"

Lucian muttered in his sleep again.

"Shhh," Martin hissed again frantically.

"What if the rat comes back, Martin? What if—"

"It won't. *It won't.*" Martin sounded as if he were about to burst into tears. He sounded terrified.

"Martin?"

"Please. We'll talk about it tomorrow. I promise," Martin whispered tearfully. "But we can't talk anymore tonight."

"Why not, Martin? What are you afraid of?"

"Nothing," said Martin. "But it's late. And dark . . . tomorrow, okay, Jeep?"

"Tomorrow," said Jeep. "Or else."

• • •

Jeep frowned down at the letter he'd just written to his parents. He wanted out of Camp Westerra. Would they come and rescue him?

Then he had another thought. What if they didn't believe him?

"You're up early." William's shadow fell across Jeep's bed. Jeep folded the letter in half quickly. He put it in the envelope, sealed the envelope, and stuck the stamp on.

"Am I?" he asked. He nodded toward Martin's empty bunk. "Martin already left for the bathhouse."

At least that was where Jeep thought Martin was. Martin had been gone when Jeep woke up. Jeep suspected that Martin was trying to avoid him. But he wasn't going to let Martin get away with it.

Across the cabin Lucian slept on, his blankets pulled up over his head.

William said, "Letter to your parents. What a good boy you are."

Jeep shrugged. He figured it would get on William's nerves.

He was right. William frowned. "Did you promise your mommy and daddy you'd send them a letter every day? Did you tell them all about the big, mean, nasty rat that gave their little boy a nightmare?"

Jeep stuck the envelope into the pocket of his jeans. "You've got something gross stuck in your teeth," he told William.

William jumped back. "You're so funny I forgot to

48

laugh, Holmes." He turned and slammed out of the cabin.

Lucian didn't move.

The wake-up bell began to clang. Jeep figured it was safe to go to the bathhouse now. Whatever was lurking outside wouldn't make a move in such a big crowd of kids.

He hoped.

The cabin door opened, and Martin came in.

"Aha," said Jeep.

Martin jumped and gave Jeep a guilty look.

"Martin," Jeep said. "Let's talk rats. Or bats. What about bats? Or maybe we could talk about all the other mega-weird, creepshow stuff that I think is going on at this camp."

"Shhh," said Martin. He nodded in the direction of Lucian's bed.

"He's dead to the world," said Jeep.

"Not now. We can't talk now. We haven't got time," said Martin, licking his lips. He hurried across the room. "Hey. Lucian. Wake up," he said.

Lucian didn't answer.

Martin kicked the side of Lucian's bed with his foot. "Wake up," he repeated.

Lucian still didn't move.

"Hey! Lucian." Martin reached out and grabbed Lucian's shoulder. Lucian flopped over onto his back, and the blanket fell away from around his ears.

Martin froze. His mouth opened soundlessly. His eyes bulged out.

"Martin?" said Jeep, a sudden chill going up his backbone.

Martin began to back slowly away from Lucian's bunk. "What is it, Martin?"

Martin pointed. His mouth closed and opened again, like a fish's mouth.

Jeep jumped up. He grabbed Martin's arm and gave it a shake. "Cut it out," he said.

"Lu-Lu-cian," Martin stammered. His glasses slid down his nose. Sweat popped out on his forehead. His cheeks had turned pale.

But not as pale as Lucian. Lucian's face was a colorless mask. Deep purple circles made half-moons beneath Lucian's closed eyes. His whole body was as stiff as a board.

"He . . . he's *dead!*" shrieked Martin. "Lucian's dead!"

CHAPTER
6

"No," said Jeep.

He heard voices outside the cabin door.

"No," he said again.

"Dead," wailed Martin. "Dead, dead, dead!"

"Stop that!" Pete ordered, slamming open the cabin door. "Act like a camper!"

Martin stopped in midscream, his eyes meeting Pete's. "B-But he's—"

Pete pushed Martin and Jeep to one side. He leaned over Lucian's motionless body. He put his hand on Lucian's forehead.

In spite of himself Jeep shuddered. He'd never touched a dead body before.

"Is he really dead?" William said from behind them.

Jeep was shocked at the tone of William's voice. It was so cold. "Isn't . . . wasn't . . . Lucian your friend?" he asked.

William ignored Jeep. "So, is he? Dead?" William asked Pete.

Pete finally lifted his hand from Lucian's forehead. He pulled the blanket up to Lucian's chin.

"This is *camp*," Martin whimpered, his glasses fogging up. "This isn't supposed to happen."

"Shut up, Martin," said William. He was staring at Lucian, too. He looked horrified. And fascinated.

And Lucian really did look dead.

Pete said, "William. There's a phone in my cabin. Go call the director. Tell him to send Nurse Hatchett to the Bear Outpost, Purple Bear, right away."

"But—," William said.

"Do it," said Pete. "*Now.*"

As William turned and rushed out of the cabin, Jeep's eyes met Martin's.

Jeep wondered if Martin had noticed what he had noticed: two tiny red marks just below Lucian's ear.

Marks like the toothmarks of a giant rat.

Or something worse. Something much, much worse.

"So you killed off one of your bunkmates!" shouted Dawn across the crowded mess hall.

Everyone instantly fell silent. What felt like a million pairs of eyes turned toward Jeep and Martin.

"No," Jeep muttered. He grabbed a tray and headed for the mess-hall line. Behind him Martin did the same. Martin had been sticking to Jeep like glue ever since Renfield and Nurse Hatchett had carried Lucian's limp form up the trail on a stretcher.

Without looking at what he was getting to eat, Jeep pushed his way down the line and then to the nearest table. Martin followed him like a shadow. Martin's hands were shaking visibly as he put down his tray.

Jeep was meanly pleased to see that his own hands were quite steady.

"So did you kill him? Or what?" Dawn plopped down in the chair across from them.

"Go away, Dawn. No one asked you to sit down," said Jeep.

"He's not dead," Martin gasped. "It's the flu. Or something. That's what Nurse Hatchett said."

"That's not what I heard. I heard you thought he was dead, Martin." Dawn pretended to clutch her throat and said in a high, loud voice, "Dead, ooooh, he's dead!"

People nearby snickered. A flush rose under Martin's sunburned cheeks. He lowered his head and stuffed a piece of zucchini bread in his mouth, a nauseated expression on his face.

Dawn turned her attention to Jeep. "Did Lucian really look dead? What did he look like?"

"Unhealthy," said Jeep. "Unwell. Sick. Like you. Okay?"

"Ha, ha." Dawn jerked her head in William's direction. William was sitting a few tables away. He was chewing ferociously, staring out the window. He wasn't talking to the others at his table. He was ignoring them.

"William's taking it pretty hard," Dawn said, lowering her voice. "I've never seen him so shook up."

"How can you tell?" Jeep muttered.

Martin said, "What about *me*? I found him. It was awful."

"So what *did* Lucian look like? Dead? Completely, you know, dead?"

"He's not dead!" Jeep said.

Staring at Dawn, Martin said, "He was pale. Really, really pale. He had these big circles under his eyes. And when I touched him, he felt as cold as ice."

"That's dead," said Dawn in a satisfied tone of voice.

"He's *not* dead!" Jeep's voice rose. Several people turned to stare. More snickers followed.

I've got to stop doing that, thought Jeep.

"And he . . . ," Martin was going on. "He had . . ." Martin's hand rose involuntarily to his neck.

Jeep kicked Martin hard under the table.

"Owwwww," said Martin. He gave Jeep a hurt look.

"Martin doesn't feel like talking about it anymore," said Jeep.

"No, that's okay. I—"

"So he's not going to talk about it anymore," said Jeep, glaring at Martin.

Martin got the hint. Finally. "Oh," he said. "Yeah. That's it. That's all."

Dawn turned her sharp gaze from Jeep to Martin. "That's not all, is it?"

Neither Jeep nor Martin answered her. Jeep stared at her hard. Martin stared down at his plate.

"I *knew* something was going on," she said. "And I'm going to find out what it is." She jumped to her feet and walked away.

For the first time all day Martin was alone with Jeep. *If you can call sitting across the table from someone in the middle of the mess hall being alone,* thought Jeep.

He looked at Martin. Martin was watching William. Behind Martin's thick glasses one *eye* was twitching. In fact, Martin looked twitchy all over. Martin was definitely losing it.

"Martin," said Jeep, trying to sound normal.

Martin turned to face Jeep.

"We have to talk," said Jeep.

Martin's whole body seemed to twitch. "Not here!" he gasped. "Not in the middle of all these people. Everybody's watching!"

"It's the best place," said Jeep. "Everybody's watching us, but nobody—except Dawn—is coming near us. Or haven't you noticed?"

Martin's eyes darted around wildly.

"They expect us to talk, Martin. It looks more suspicious if we don't. Besides, no one can sneak up on us, either. Just keep your voice down. Okay? Martin? Martin, are you in there?"

For a moment Jeep thought Martin had completely

lost it. Then Martin slowly stopped twitching. He focused on Jeep and took a deep breath. He nodded. "Okay," he said hoarsely.

"Good." Lowering his voice and watching carefully to make sure no one came close enough to the two of them to overhear anything, Jeep said, as calmly as he could, "Martin, you know what's going on here, don't you?"

"No!" gasped Martin.

"Yes you do," said Jeep. "You know. You've known from the beginning. You've figured it out, the same as I have, haven't you?"

"No, I tell you."

"The counselors are all pale and weird. They hate the sun. They wear their dark glasses all the time."

"S-So?"

"The camp director keeps bats, Martin. *Bats.*"

"Bats are good animals," said Martin weakly.

"I agree. Most bats. But not these *particular* bats. You know why, don't you, Martin?"

"No!"

"And how about this, Martin. The rat—the giant rat—was after me last night. Just like the bats were after me. And maybe after you, Martin. Have you thought about that? Maybe you just got lucky, too. And Lucian got unlucky."

"Nooooo," moaned Martin.

"Yes, Martin." Jeep leaned so close to Martin that he could see the pores of Martin's sweaty face. "It's true. It's all true. The director of this camp is a vampire. And

I think most of the counselors are, too. And maybe even some of the campers.''

Although he didn't say anything, Martin kept moaning. *Martin,* thought Jeep, *is not my first choice for help.*

But then what choice do I have?

When Jeep had finished talking, Martin said, "Blood. Crows. Rats. . . .''

"Or the same rat," said Jeep. "Something was following me last night, I tell you. Something's been out to get me ever since I got to Camp Westerra.''

Martin moaned again. "It can't be true.''

"Or maybe something is out to get all of us.''

"But why?'' said Martin. His voice got shrill.

"Shhh!'' said Jeep. "We need to go see Lucian. We need to talk to him. Maybe he can tell us what happened to him.''

"I don't want to see Lucian," said Martin.

Jeep ignored him. He stood up, picked up his tray and walked out of the mess hall.

"Where are you going?'' Martin whimpered. "Don't leave me!''

"I'm going to mail my letter," Jeep said loudly in case anyone was listening. He pointed at the wooden mailbox on the porch of the camp headquarters.

Jeep walked to the mailbox with Martin at his heels. He stuck the letter in the mailbox. He looked over his shoulder. Camp Westerra looked peaceful in the noonday sun. A pleasant sort of buzz came from the mess

57

hall, where some kids were still finishing lunch. Others had begun to drift toward their cabins for the postlunch rest period.

The sun sparkled off the dark lake. The camp flag fluttered in the breeze.

"Come on!" growled Jeep, and dragged Martin around the side of the camp headquarters toward the infirmary.

"Where are you going *now*?" Martin whined.

"Chill out, Martin. I'm going to see Lucian."

"I don't want to see Lucian. Besides, Pete told us that he couldn't have visitors for at least a day."

"A day is too late, Martin. In fact we may be too late already," Jeep said.

They stopped outside the screen door of the infirmary. Voices sounded on the other side of the door. Someone was laughing. Several people were applauding.

"That's not the answer, stupid," said an irritable voice.

Martin stopped twitching. "She has a television," he said, outraged. "We're not even allowed to have our Walkmans, and Nurse Hatchett has a television."

"Get a grip, Martin," said Jeep. "And *be quiet.*"

"Aorta," the nurse practitioner shouted at the television. "The answer is 'aorta,' you ignorant biped!"

Jeep peered through the door. Nurse Hatchett was sitting in a small room to one side of the hall in a reclining chair. She had her nurse's cap on her knee. Her back was to the door, and she was watching a game show on television.

Quickly and quietly Jeep pushed the door open and crept past the nurse to the only other room in the infirmary. It had three narrow beds in it. Two of them were empty. In the last one Lucian lay quietly, staring up at the ceiling.

The room was very dark. A sliver of daylight came through a crack in the curtains.

Jeep dragged Martin into the room behind him, then shut the door as softly as possible.

"Lucian," he said, "we've got to talk to you."

For a moment Lucian stayed motionless. For a moment Jeep thought Lucian really *was* dead. Then Lucian slowly turned his head to face Jeep and Martin.

"You," he whispered. "It's all your fault!"

"Lucian, what are you talking about?" asked Jeep. He walked over to stand by Lucian's bed.

Lucian's gaze fastened on Jeep. For a moment he didn't seem to recognize Jeep. Then his eyes widened. He said, "Jeep. I'm sorry. I—"

Martin interrupted. "Nurse Hatchett is going to hear us!"

"We have to hurry," Jeep agreed. "Lucian, what happened to you?"

Frowning, Lucian said, "Happened? I got sick. Like the flu, the doctor said. I'll be okay again in another day."

He smiled weakly up at Jeep. It was a gruesome sight. His teeth looked too big for his mouth.

"Stop smiling," begged Martin.

Lucian stopped smiling. He looked puzzled.

Jeep waved at Martin to be quiet. "Lucian, was it the rat? Do you remember the rat? *Did the rat bite you?*"

"Rat?" Lucian winced as if the thought hurt. He turned his head away. "I don't feel good. You should go now."

Jeep bent forward, squinting at Lucian, examining his neck. The two little red marks he'd seen that morning were gone.

Gone.

Just like that.

Now there were only two tiny, shiny-white scars.

"Go away," Lucian said. He turned back toward the two boys, and his eyes burned. "Go play in the sun."

"Lucian," Jeep said urgently.

"He can't help us. He can't remember anything," said Martin.

"It was the rat, wasn't it, Lucian?" said Jeep. "You know it was. And you know why, don't you, Lucian? You know it wasn't really a rat, don't you, Lucian? *Don't you?*"

Lucian slowly turned his head back toward Jeep. He licked his dry lips. Suddenly his hand shot out and gripped the front of Jeep's shirt. Despite his deathly appearance Lucian's grip was incredibly strong.

He pulled Jeep toward him. His lips moved.

"Rat . . . ," he muttered. "I—"

Martin grabbed Jeep's arm and yanked him back.

But Lucian didn't let go. He stared deeply into Jeep's eyes. Suddenly Jeep's knees felt weak. He thought he was going to faint. And he was so cold. So very cold. . . .

"Rat . . . ," gasped Lucian. He drew his lips back in a terrible grin. "Bloooooood . . ."

"No!" shouted Martin. He yanked at Jeep with all his might.

But Jeep braced himself and leaned toward Lucian.

"Bloood," whispered Lucian desperately.

Martin let go of Jeep's arm and lunged for the curtain. He yanked it open.

Light fell across Lucian. He gave a strangled cry and let go of Jeep.

Lucian seemed to grow smaller in his bed. He twisted and turned, sitting up and looking past Jeep. His eyes widened, then rolled up in his head. "Noooo," he moaned, and fell back with a thud.

CHAPTER
7

The room grew colder. And very, very still.

Jeep turned. Martin's face was bright red. His eyes were bulging out behind his glasses. He was pointing toward the door of the room and trying to speak.

She was huge. She filled the whole doorway of the hospital room. She was dressed all in dreadful, icy white. Except for her dark glasses.

She folded her arms. "Aha," she said. "I thought I smelled a rat!"

Jeep didn't bother to look at Martin. He knew without turning his head that all he would see was Martin twitching. Martin was hopeless. It was up to Jeep.

He cleared his throat. He thought of several things he could say. Like "Trick or treat." Or "Hey, Halloween's not until October."

But somehow he didn't think she'd laugh.

Somehow he didn't think she was human.

Jeep forced himself to smile. "Hi!" he said. "We just came to visit Lucian. We're in his cabin. He got sick last night, and we wanted to make sure he was okay."

The dark glasses turned from Jeep to Martin and back to Jeep. "He's fine," said the nurse. She added, "He can't have visitors. After all, you wouldn't want to catch what he's got, would you, boys?"

"No!" shouted Martin.

"I thought not," said Nurse Hatchett. She stepped to one side and motioned for Jeep and Martin to leave.

Jeep allowed himself a quick glance in Lucian's direction. Lucian's eyes were closed. His body was rigid beneath the sheets.

"Are you sure it's just the flu?" Jeep said. "I mean, what's wrong with him? Shouldn't he go to a hospital or something?"

In answer the nurse walked stiffly past Jeep and pulled the curtains shut. "He's fine," she said in an expressionless voice. "These things run their course in a day or two. By tomorrow he'll feel like his old self again." She paused. She tilted her head. Then she added, "Maybe even better.

"But meanwhile we don't want him to have visitors because we don't want anyone else catching it. So I suggest that if you know what's good for you, you leave. *Immediately.*"

Martin grabbed Jeep's sleeve. "S-S-Sure," he stuttered. "No problem."

Reluctantly Jeep allowed himself to be pulled out of the room. As Martin dragged him out of the front door of the infirmary, Jeep looked over his shoulder. The last thing he saw was the nurse, standing in the doorway of Lucian's room, the sweater thrown over her shoulders outlined against the darkened room behind her like the wings of a giant bat.

The mess hall was cheerfully lit in the dusk of early evening. The campers fell into line to go inside.

Jeep tried to act cool. Martin's jumping and twitching and frightened face were not helping things.

Great, thought Jeep. *The only person I trust at this whole camp and he's even more afraid than I am.*

Not that I'm scared, he thought. *I can handle this.*

But it didn't help that he was at a camp all alone in the middle of the woods. It didn't help that it was getting dark. It didn't help that he had another night ahead of him.

Up ahead he heard Nora's voice. "Grow *up,* Dawn," she said.

Dawn laughed her weird, cracked laugh.

Dawn, thought Jeep. Dawn, the wonder woman of the woods.

Maybe Dawn could help. He wasn't quite sure how, but he pushed ahead. He grabbed Dawn by the arm.

"Hey, let go!" Dawn spun around, her fist raised, her eyes blazing. Then she saw Jeep. "Oh. It's you."

Nora said, "Hi, Jeep." She giggled and smoothed back her hair. Another girl leaned over and whispered in Nora's ear, and they both giggled.

Trying to ignore them, Jeep said, "Hi, Dawn. How are you doing?"

"Fine." Dawn gave Jeep a puzzled look. Then her eyes narrowed. "Killed any more Bear campers?"

Martin tentatively raised his hand to wave.

"Oh, hi, Martin," Dawn added.

"I need to talk to you," said Jeep.

A sly look crossed Dawn's face. "Like about what happened to poor Lucian?" she asked.

They had almost reached the door of the cafeteria. Jeep stepped out of line and pulled Dawn and Martin with him. He moved away until they were standing in the shadows at the far end of the porch.

"What? What?" Dawn asked. "What is it? You can tell me! I promise!"

"If you'll stop talking, I *will* tell you," said Jeep.

"It's not true," babbled Martin. "It's just a theory. I mean, we don't have any proof—"

"Shhh," said Jeep. He looked around the corner of the porch to make sure no one was standing there. He leaned over the railing to make sure no one was crouched in the shadows below.

Dawn said impatiently, "What's going on, Jeep?"

For a moment Jeep hesitated. But what did he have to lose? He lowered his voice and said one word, softly:

"Vampires."

• • •

He expected Dawn to laugh her weird laugh. He expected her to put her hands on her hips and tell him he was crazy.

He expected Martin to moan and groan and wring his hands.

Martin moaned and groaned and wrung his hands.

But Dawn just stared at Jeep. She just stood there, a dark shadow on the dark porch. Behind them campers laughed and talked and pushed their way into the dining hall.

Jeep looked up at the sky. He'd noticed them before, but he'd never registered them until now: black wheeling flecks against the summer-bright night, like bits of ash blown in the wind. But they weren't bits of ash.

They were bats.

He lowered his gaze. Dawn still hadn't spoken. Martin was clutching his head as if it hurt.

Then Dawn nodded. "Vampires," she said with deep satisfaction. "Tell me *everything*."

Quickly Jeep told her what had been happening since he'd gotten to camp, beginning with the splinter in his thumb and ending with the visit to Lucian.

"They've got Lucian," he said. "I'm almost sure he's been turned into a vampire. But there's still time to save everybody else."

The last of the campers were going into the mess hall. The counselors would notice them in a minute. They didn't have much time.

Dawn said, "So the counselors, led by Renfield, lure unsuspecting campers to Camp Westerra and turn them into vampires."

"No," said Martin. "Not me!"

"Yes. Exactly," said Jeep.

"We need to get proof. Then we can get help," said Dawn.

Without seeming to realize it, Dawn turned the collar up on her rugby shirt. "Vampires," she said almost to herself. "The undead. Which makes this camp a sort of Club Dead. Get it?"

"It's not funny," said Jeep.

Dawn said, suddenly solemn, "I know. I guess I make jokes when I'm scared."

"You're not scared, are you?" Jeep felt a momentary surge of panic.

There was a little silence. Martin moaned to himself. Dawn and Jeep stared at each other. Then Dawn tossed her head. "Of course I'm not," she said.

"Not hungry?" said a smooth, disembodied voice.

"Wh-What?" Martin yelped.

Renfield materialized in the darkness beside the porch. *How does he do that?* thought Jeep.

Then he thought, *He's a vampire, dummy. It's easy.*

"I said, are you not hungry?" intoned Renfield.

"Sure," said Dawn. "Sure I am."

"The dinner line is over there," said Renfield.

"Right," said Jeep. "Well, guys, let's go chow." He

walked quickly away from Renfield. He could feel the hair on his neck standing up.

"We need to talk more," said Dawn under the cover of clattering dishes and silverware as they went down the dinner line. "We need to get proof. We need to do research. A good camper is always prepared." She said the last sentence as if it were a good-luck charm.

"I'm not a good camper," said Jeep.

"You will be. Or—if what you're saying is true—we'll all be dead."

"Or worse," said Jeep.

"Or worse," agreed Dawn, picking up her tray and leading the way into the dining hall of the undead.

CHAPTER
8

"Seen Lucian?" William asked.

"L-Lucian?" Martin sat down heavily on his bunk bed. The springs creaked in protest.

William sat down on the edge of his bed and stuck his finger in his ear. "Yeah. I went up to see him and that Hatchett nurse practitioner said he's getting out tomorrow. Said it was just a bug that was going around. Like a cold." He took his finger out of his ear and inspected it. He made a face. "Hope I don't get it."

"Me too," said Martin fervently.

Jeep didn't say anything. The sight of William searching for ear jam would once have grossed him totally out. But now it barely moved him. William was gross. William was dumb. But William was the least of his worries.

Stretching out on his bed, Jeep folded his hands under his head and stared at the rafters. He and Martin had agreed to take turns staying awake and keeping watch all night.

It was Jeep's turn to sleep first, but he didn't think he'd be able to. William began excavating the other ear. Jeep got up and put on a turtleneck sweater, pulling it up as high as it would go. He closed his eyes.

Jeep hoped Martin could be trusted. He was pretty sure Martin was scared enough to stay awake.

What would happen if they told William? he wondered. He opened his eyes slightly and peered through the slits.

Would William believe them? Or would he think they were crazy? William didn't seem to have much of an imagination. He was probably the type that wanted proof. Real evidence.

Like being turned into a vampire.

But that wouldn't happen as long as Martin and Jeep were on watch.

He wondered how Dawn was going to hold out.

Proof. Taps sounded over the loudspeakers mounted on top of the camp headquarters. Renfield lived at the camp headquarters. So did his bats. He let them out at night.

Did he go out with them? Vampires could take the shapes of other animals, particularly bats and rats. . . .

But could they take the shape of, say, campers? Or camp counselors? He had a sudden image of all the camp counselors—all those pale people in caps and shades, wincing around in the sun and frying like fish in spite of a sea of sunscreen.

Vampires couldn't take the sun. But they were out in

it—even if they weren't happy about it. Were they vampires? Or vampires' helpers of some sort?

Or was he going completely crazy?

No. And tomorrow he was going to find a way of proving that he wasn't. A way of stopping the vampires.

All he had to do now was make it through the night.

The sound of a bugle playing the morning wake-up call blared over the loudspeaker.

Jeep awoke with a start. He was sitting up at the end of his bed, slumped against the wall, his flashlight clutched in one hand.

He hadn't been asleep! He couldn't have slept! It was his turn to keep watch.

Jerking upright, he surveyed the room by the dawn's pale, anemic light. Funny how the early-morning sun seemed to drain all the color out of everything, all the life. Everything looked gray. It made him tired just to look at it.

He put his hands up to his neck. Relief surged through him. His turtleneck was still pulled up practically over his ears.

Of course it was, he told himself. *You haven't been asleep that long.* The first light of morning had already begun to outline the windows before he'd dozed off. And he hadn't been sleeping that heavily. He would have heard the door open, heard it knock against the metal canteen filled with rocks that he'd propped against it.

73

Good. The canteen was still there. He heard one of the other cabin doors slam. It was a reassuring sound. He got out of bed quietly and picked up the canteen and slid it under his bed.

More cabin doors slammed. He heard voices. The Bear Outpost was waking up.

Rubbing his eyes and yawning, he got up and went over to grab Martin's shoulder.

"Time to get up," he said in a low voice.

Martin slept on, like a big lump.

"Yo, Martin. Rise and shine. We've got a busy day," said Jeep. He looked over his shoulder, expecting to see William bouncing up out of his bunk. William was usually the first up. He was the Perfect Camper, making his bed before he ever left the cabin and headed for the bathroom.

This morning, though, William was still asleep, too.

Jeep grabbed Martin's shoulder and shook harder. Martin rolled over. But he didn't squint up at Jeep. He didn't groan in sleepy protest.

He just lay there. Very still. Very still. And very, very cold.

Jeep stepped back. Keeping his eyes on Martin, he backed up until he bumped against William's bed.

William flopped over. His eyes stayed closed. His mouth sagged open in a horrible way. There were two tiny red marks just below his right ear.

"No!" Jeep said in a strangled whisper. He raced back

to Martin's bunk. He grabbed Martin by both shoulders. "Martin! Speak to me! Martin! Please! Martin!"

Martin's head rolled back. His eyes were rolled up in his head.

Two tiny red marks dotted his neck just below his right ear.

Martin and William were both dead.

Or worse.

The vampires had gotten them. They were undead.

With a wild shriek of terror Jeep ran from the cabin and out into the clearing at the middle of the Bear Outpost.

"Help me! Help me!" he screamed. "They got Martin! They got William! The vampires are coming! *The vampires* are com—"

He stopped in midshriek as his fellow campers all turned toward him. One by one they began to smile. He saw their terrible pointed fangs. He saw their eyes turn hungry red behind their evil dark glasses.

It was too late. The vampires had gotten them all.

And he was next. . . .

"Shhh!"

A hand clamped over his mouth. He twisted and tried to breathe. His fist lashed out and hit something.

The hand let go. "Ooof," Martin said in an angry whisper. "What'dja have to do that for, Jeep? It's just me!"

Jeep's eyes opened.

It was Martin. "How can you sleep at a time like this?" Martin complained. "It's your turn to keep watch."

"Martin!" Jeep gasped.

"Just don't fall asleep, okay?" said Martin crossly. He went back to his bunk.

Jeep sat up, his heart pounding so hard, he thought he was going to be sick. It had all been a bad dream. Or at least the part about the whole camp turning into vampires had been.

But it could come true.

They were in worse danger than he'd ever realized. It was up to them to save the camp.

Before it was too late.

CHAPTER

9

"You look terrible!"

"You don't look so great yourself," Jeep answered Dawn.

Nora, who had drifted up to stand behind Dawn, giggled. "Do you want me to save you a place for breakfast, Dawn?"

Giving Nora an annoyed look, Dawn said, "Isn't that what you usually do?"

"Wellll . . ." Nora cocked her head to one side and looked at Jeep in what Jeep thought was a particularly goofy way. "I thought you might want to sit with someone else."

"If you keep acting dumb, I will," retorted Dawn.

Nora nudged Dawn with her shoulder and, with another giggle, went into the dining hall.

"We're all still here," said Martin brightly. "That's good."

"We need proof," said Jeep.

77

Martin nodded. "Knowledge is power," he said seriously.

Jeep groaned, but Dawn nodded, too. "We have to figure out how to stop these guys. Which means we have to learn everything we can about them. Research. Information gathering."

"Spying," said Jeep.

"Yep," said Dawn. She went on, "I vote Martin in charge of the research. He can go up to the camp library. Maybe it has some books or computer stuff that could help us."

"I could do that," said Martin, looking pleased and a little less haggard. He scratched at his nose, which was starting to peel.

Some other kids passed them. "What did the plate say to the knife?" one of them asked, and then answered his own question. "Oh, you're such a cutup."

Once I would have said that was funny. Stupid, but funny, thought Jeep.

But not anymore, he realized. The time for joking was past. It was a matter of life and death. Unless they all wanted to be next on the menu—as the vampire special.

"And I'm in charge of field maneuvers," said Dawn.

Jeep made a face.

"I know my way around the woods, which is more than you do," said Dawn.

"Did I say anything?" asked Jeep. "Did I argue?" Dawn was a big pain, but she did know her way around the woods. He didn't have much choice. Jeep looked at

Dawn and Martin. "Okay. Now, we have to keep our eyes open. Watch our backs . . . and our necks. Don't take chances. And try not to act as if you suspect any-thing . . . like we'd better get to breakfast now, or people will wonder why we're always hanging around whisper-ing."

"Don't worry." Dawn suddenly laughed. "Nora thinks you have a crush on me. I'll just tell her it's true."

She laughed her maniacal laugh and turned and walked into the mess hall.

"Great," said Jeep, glaring after Dawn. "This is all I need."

"Is it true, Jeep?" Martin said, his eyes round behind his glasses. "Do you have a crush on Dawn?"

Jeep groaned.

"Nice work, Jeep." The counselor bent over him. Jeep looked up and froze. She wasn't wearing her dark glasses. Why wasn't she wearing her dark glasses? All the counselors *always* wore their dark glasses.

But she wasn't. Her eyes glowed beneath the black fringe of her bangs. The blue irises were like bits of pale blue glass. Jeep felt as if they were looking inside his head. Vampires weren't mind readers—were they?

"Is something wrong, Jeep?" asked the counselor softly. She put her hand on his shoulder. It felt as cold as ice through his cotton T-shirt. "You can tell me."

Jeep felt himself weakening.

He felt his strength draining away.

He tried not to look into her eyes.

He couldn't help himself.

"Jeep? Oh, Jeep . . . ," a singsong voice said.

Nearby he heard Nora's familiar giggle. "Jeep has a girlfriend," she said in a loud whisper. The two girls next to her began to laugh, too.

For once Jeep was glad.

He managed to tear his gaze from the counselor's frozen eyes. He thought he saw an expression of annoyance cross her face as he spun away to glare at Nora. But he couldn't be sure.

He took a deep breath. *Act normal,* he told himself. "Are you crazy?" he practically snarled at Nora. "Why don't you just go tell it on *Oprah*?"

"Well, excuuuse me," said Nora, giggling even more.

With a snort of disgust Jeep looked down at the animal mask he was making. He tried to gather his thoughts. He wondered how Nora would feel if she knew that he was glad of what she'd said.

If it hadn't been for Nora, he might have broken down. Told the counselor everything.

He stared at the papier-mâché mask of his own face. He was using it as the base for a bear mask. He needed to decorate it. He needed to act normal. Interested in what he was doing. Like a typical camper. He reached for the brown paint.

A little while later the door of the crafts studio banged open. Martin came hurrying in and sat down next to Jeep.

"Find what you were looking for, Martin?" the counselor asked. The way she looked at Martin didn't seem as creepy as the way she'd looked at Jeep. In fact, it seemed perfectly normal and friendly.

Boy, they're good at acting normal, thought Jeep. *Big saber-toothed creeps.*

"Uh, yeah, thanks," said Martin. "I, uh, sketched some designs for my mask. From a book. You know." He looked at the counselor apprehensively, but she just nodded and moved down the table.

"So what'dja find?" Jeep asked softly.

Martin picked up his own mask and began to poke at it.

"I wrote it up for Dawn," he said out of the side of his mouth. He slid his fist down the table toward Jeep and laid a tightly folded piece of paper next to Jeep's hand. Quickly Jeep covered the piece of paper with his own hand and slid it off the table into his pocket.

Martin lowered his voice and leaned close to Jeep. "It's all true," he whispered. "They drink blood. They can turn their victims into vampires by doing that if they want to. Or just kill them."

Holding his mask up to his face and pretending to make some adjustments, Jeep nodded. He peered out through the slits of the eyes, watching over Martin's shoulder to make sure no one was sneaking up on them or trying to listen. Martin was doing the same for Jeep, his eyes darting from left to right.

"Go on," Jeep said.

"Well, they can't eat real food. Makes 'em sick. Don't have reflections. Probably don't show up in photographs." Martin permitted himself a small smile. "Have *you* ever seen a photograph of a vampire?"

"Only in the movies," Jeep cracked. They both snickered. But their laughter only lasted a moment.

Then Martin went on. "They have superhuman strength. They have the power to change shape. They prefer to turn into bats and rats, but they can do other animals. They have power over all kinds of other animals: wolves, cats . . . and of course bats and rats."

"Terrific," muttered Jeep.

Martin took a deep breath. "And there aren't a whole lot of ways to stop them. You can wear garlic around your neck. That's supposed to keep them away, although not everybody believes that. Other methods include stakes through the heart, burning, exposure to the sun. . . ."

"You found all that in the camp library? Good work," said Jeep.

Martin gave a modest shrug.

"It's not gonna be easy getting proof," said Jeep. "We need to talk to Dawn." He looked down at the folded piece of paper. He looked over at where Nora was sitting with her girlfriends. With a sigh Jeep unfolded the note. "Meet me after dinner behind the dining hall," he wrote at the bottom. He folded the note back up. Then, just to be safe, he got some glue and glued it shut. He walked over to Nora. "Can you give this to Dawn for me?" Jeep asked, trying to sound casual.

Nora took the note and gave Jeep a sly look. "A note for Dawn," she said loudly. "Sure, Jeep. I'd be *glad* to."

They were still giggling as Jeep walked back to his seat.

He sat down across from Martin. Martin looked at Nora. He looked back at Jeep. "Don't say anything," Jeep warned.

Martin kept his mouth shut.

Jeep said, "It's a dirty job. But somebody's gotta do it."

Jeep was watching the campers clear off their tables after dinner while Mr. Renfield made announcements.

"And senior campers, don't forget, tonight is the big night: the senior campfire, to initiate the new senior campers joining our little Camp Westerra family."

Many of the campers, Jeep noticed grimly, had barely touched their food. Mostly the senior campers, it seemed. Oh, the mashed potatoes had been stirred around and the rolls broken up into bits, to make it look as if food had been eaten. But Jeep was familiar with that technique. Most of the students at Graveyard School had used it at one time or another, especially during the recent, mercifully brief reign of a strange new lunchroom superintendent.

Martin's appetite seemed undiminished. In fact, he was cramming rolls into his pockets. "To keep my strength up," he told Jeep.

Jeep emptied his own tray into the garbage can and headed for the dining-hall door. Were most of the seniors vampires already?

Then a sudden thought made his blood run cold. Was tonight's initiation going to turn more unsuspecting campers into vampires? Was that what it meant to be a senior camper?

Ahead of them Nora pulled a small mirror out of her pocket and held it up. She examined her face in it and smoothed her bangs. She grabbed Dawn's arm and thrust the mirror toward her.

Dawn frowned. Nora nodded significantly in Jeep's direction. She handed Dawn a comb.

Reluctantly Dawn took the mirror. She held it up and rolled her eyes. Walking up behind them, Jeep saw a blur of movement in the small mirror Dawn was holding.

Then suddenly Dawn whipped around. Her eyes widened as she looked at Jeep. The color drained from her face.

She half turned, and thrust the mirror back at Nora and almost threw the comb at her.

Nora looked puzzled. Then she turned, too, and saw Jeep and Martin, and the puzzled look left her face. Quickly she pocketed the mirror.

"Not sneaking out, are you?" said a smooth voice behind Jeep.

Pete came up to join them.

Nora predictably giggled. "We're just going out on the porch," she explained.

84

Dawn didn't say anything. She looked stunned. Jeep said quickly, "For some fresh air."

"Well, don't wander off," said Pete. "We're going to be meeting to plan our skits for the camp show."

"What show?" asked Jeep.

Pete punched Jeep on the arm. Hard. "You'll see," he said.

As Pete walked away, Nora suddenly squealed, "Martin! I wanted to ask you something!"

"Wh-What?" Martin took a step back. But it was too late. Nora had his arm. She began to drag Martin away. "See you later," she said meaningfully to Dawn. "Bye-bye, Jeep," she added coyly.

It was so obvious. Nora was dragging Martin away so that Dawn and Jeep could be alone together.

It made Jeep want to throw up.

Martin looked desperately back over his shoulder at Jeep. Jeep almost felt sorry for Martin.

But they had a job to do, Jeep reminded himself sternly. "It's okay, Martin," he said. "I'll catch you later."

Dawn still hadn't spoken.

"C'mon," said Jeep. "Let's get out of here." He led the way outside. They went over to a bend under a tree near the front door of the mess hall.

Jeep sat down. Dawn sat down, too.

"You got my note?" he said.

Dawn turned her head slowly. She nodded slightly.

"Nora didn't see it, did she?"

Dawn shook her head.

"Good." Jeep took a deep breath, thinking about the senior campfire. The initiation. The night's work that was ahead.

Sneaking through the woods. Spying on vampires.

Alone in the woods with vampires. . . .

He decided to break it to her gently. "I'm afraid I have some bad news," he said.

"I know," said Dawn.

"You do?"

"Yes," she said. A slight tremor seemed to go through her body. She stopped it. She took a deep breath.

"You saw it, too," she said. "Didn't you?"

"It's only the senior campers, mostly," said Jeep. "And the counselors, of course. But I still think we can—"

"What are you talking about?" Dawn's voice rose.

"Shhh! About the way all the seniors don't eat. They just pretend to eat. Don't you get it? It's because they're vampires . . . and we have to go to the senior campfire tonight because I think they're going to be initiating the new senior campers—welcoming new vampires. We can get our proof there!"

Dawn said, "I have all the proof I need. Didn't you see it, Jeep? When Pete came up behind me? I could see him out of the corner of my eye. I could see him and you and Martin. And I could see all of you in the mirror Nora gave me. . . .

"Except Pete. Pete doesn't have a reflection. Pete is definitely a vampire!"

CHAPTER
10

Jeep wasn't surprised. Of course Pete was a vampire. Didn't he wear dark glasses all the time? Wasn't he completely sunburned beneath his phony tan in spite of the hats and the sunscreen?

But the thought gave him the shivers just the same. It was one thing to think that Mr. Renfield was the leader of a camp full of vampires. And to know that the adults were part of the awful vampire plot. And to suspect that the senior campers were somehow being drawn in.

But the thought of Pete, his own Bear Outpost Leader, being a vampire, gave him the chills just the same.

"He didn't see you, did he?" asked Jeep urgently. "He doesn't suspect that you know?"

"I don't think so," said Dawn. Telling Jeep what she'd seen—and hadn't seen—seemed to calm her. She took a deep breath.

"So Pete's a vampire. So what? He's not the only

vampire in the woods, right?'' she said confidently, though her voice was wavering.

"I wish you hadn't said that," complained Jeep.

Dawn shrugged. She was her old self again.

Jeep looked down at the dark, cold lake. Above it the sky was growing steadily darker as the blood-red haze of the sunset receded. He wondered if there were bats swooping up above, silently, efficiently.

He wondered if they were real bats, good, ordinary bats who ate mosquitoes and other pests and didn't bother humans.

Somehow he didn't think so.

He turned to face Dawn. Her face was a ghostly shadow in the twilight. "Okay," he said softly. "We're going on a vampire hunt tonight. Here's the plan."

Voices murmured in the darkness around them. Jeep scrambled forward through the trees, trying to stay out of sight and not make any noise.

Could vampires see in the dark? He didn't want to think about it.

He was glad that he had talked Martin out of coming with him and Dawn to spy on the campfire. Of course it hadn't been hard. Martin had been more than willing to stay behind at the Purple Bear Outpost. His job was to say that Jeep had gone back to the mess hall to look for his sweatshirt.

"If anyone asks," Jeep had said, "tell them I had to go back because it was my Camp Westerra sweatshirt."

Martin had agreed happily. He didn't seem to see how lame the story was.

Oh well, thought Jeep, squinting into the darkness. It was Martin's problem now, not his.

Beside him, Dawn stopped. She grabbed his arm and flicked off her flashlight. The beam of light was very thin. Dawn had taped over most of the surface of the light to help prevent anyone from seeing them.

"There they are," she said softly.

Ahead a flickering glow outlined the trunks of the trees, making the gnarled trunks look as if they had grimacing, horrible faces.

Get a grip, Jeep told himself. *They're just trees.* But he kept a wary eye on them just the same.

Could vampires control trees the way they could control bats and rats and wolves? Command trees to come to life and reach out and grab unwary passersby?

No.

Putting the thought firmly out of his mind, Jeep pushed forward behind Dawn. When she stopped, he slithered up beside her. The two of them straightened up slowly and peered through the screen of branches and leaves.

A campfire blazed in the middle of a large, sandy clearing. Around the campfire the senior campers sat in a huge semicircle. On the other side of the campfire stood the new senior campers.

Mr. Renfield stood beside them. Jeep gasped. It was the first time he had ever seen Mr. Renfield without his sunglasses.

Gone was the pale director beneath the pith helmet. Despite the sunburn that made a line on his forehead where the pith helmet stopped, and the two large white circles around his eyes where the sunglasses had kept the sun out, Mr. Renfield was a commanding figure. He towered above the campfire.

Of course, the fact that he was dressed all in black, with a sweeping black cloak lined in red, helped.

Mr. Renfield surveyed the campfire gathering. His eyes looked like polished black stones. The fire blazed up, and Dawn gasped and shrank back. "Look!"

The red flames danced in Mr. Renfield's dead, dark eyes.

The campers who were already senior campers had their sunglasses pushed back on top of their heads. But the new campers, the ones standing with Renfield, were all holding identical sunglasses in their hands.

Mr. Renfield raised his hands. Sparks leaped out of the fire as if the fire itself was alive. They splattered against darkness.

"Senior campers are . . . special," Mr. Renfield said. "When you arrived, you were ordinary. Afraid. Afraid of the dark. Afraid of failure. Weak. Puny. Average.

"But now. Now . . ." Renfield raised his arms again. Sparks leaped madly up toward the sky. "Now you are . . . changed. Forever. You are true members of Camp Westerra. Now you will always have a home. Now you will always belong. You have new . . . privileges. New . . . powers. You have passed many tests. You have been faithful campers. You have earned your dark glasses."

He paused and gestured. Proudly each camper put his or her sunglasses on. Proudly they all smiled.

The senior campers pulled their dark glasses on, too. They stood up. They began to applaud. And smile. Their smiles were particularly horrifying.

"No . . . ," Jeep whispered.

All the campers, every single one of them, had gleaming white fangs.

The applause went on and on.

"I'm going to be sick," said Dawn.

"Shhh," said Jeep.

At last the clapping died away. Everyone faced Renfield expectantly.

"Now, campers. You have earned your *reward*."

At the last word Mr. Renfield's voice sank to a whisper. He surveyed the campers with his burning, coal-dark eyes.

Suddenly one of the senior campers raised her head and sniffed the air. Immediately two other campers turned. "What is it?" one of them asked.

"I smell . . ." She sniffed. She turned her head. Her two dark eyes suddenly glittered red behind her dark glasses. She sniffed harder. "I smell . . ." Her eyebrows snapped together in a frown.

"She's turning in our direction," Jeep whispered frantically.

"Don't move," said Dawn. "Get *down*."

"I smell . . ." The camper opened her mouth and reached up and tapped her fang.

In spite of himself Jeep put his hands up protectively around his throat.

Other campers turned. A murmur passed down the line of campers. Now, it seemed, the entire campfire group was turned to face where Dawn and Jeep were hiding.

A forest of fangs flashed in the firelight.

"That's it," said Dawn. "I'm outta here!"

"Dawn, wai—" But it was too late. Before Jeep could stop her, Dawn had leaped to her feet.

It seemed that the fire blazed up at the same moment, lighting up the whole world—and the shadows in the bushes where Dawn and Jeep were hiding.

"Look!" someone shouted, pointing.

"Get them!" screeched someone else.

"Stop them!"

"Reward . . . ," Renfield howled.

With red eyes blazing, the senior campers moved swiftly, soundlessly, horrifyingly, toward Dawn and Jeep.

Dawn screamed, "You'll never take me alive!" She threw her flashlight at the advancing army of vampires.

It didn't even slow them down.

Jeep yanked his cap down over his face. He hoped they hadn't recognized him. Were vampires like dogs? Could they tell who someone was by the smell? Or was that werewolves?

"Come on!" Dawn shouted.

Then Jeep was running, crashing through the bushes, running into trees. Branches whipped his face.

"This way," Dawn said, panting.

The glow of the fire faded. The woods got darker. And darker.

Jeep tripped and fell forward. He grabbed Dawn.

She socked him hard in the stomach.

"Ugh," gasped Jeep. "What was that for?"

"Sorry," said Dawn. "I thought you were a vampire."

They scrambled on. "How do you know where we're going?" Jeep asked.

"Trust me," said Dawn.

How could he argue? He couldn't even breathe. He stumbled, following the sound of Dawn crashing and thrashing ahead of him as much as the shadowy outline of her form.

Then she stopped.

Jeep stopped, too. "Are we lost?"

"Shhh! Do you hear anything?"

All Jeep could hear was his own desperate, shallow breathing.

"Hold your breath for a minute," Dawn said.

Jeep tried. Holding his breath, all he could hear was the pounding of his heart in his ears.

"I think we lost them," said Dawn at last.

Jeep allowed himself to breathe again. Was it possible?

"Where are we?" he managed to ask at last.

"I think the main camp is over that way," Dawn said. He could barely see her arm pointing in the darkness. A few minutes later she said, "Yep. I was right. It's just over the hill we're climbing."

Although he still didn't understand how Dawn could tell where she was, Jeep wasn't about to argue. He was just glad to be alive. Dawn plunged ahead, over the top of the hill.

"Hey, wait for me," said Jeep.

He ran up the hill.

When he reached the top, he stopped. Suddenly he realized how quiet it was. Quiet as a graveyard.

"Dawn?" he said.

No one answered.

Below he could see the light outside the camp headquarters. Down past it, faintly, he could see where the trail to his own cabin began.

But he couldn't see Dawn anywhere.

"Dawn?" he called again, softly.

It was so quiet.

Then he knew. The feeling had come back. The feeling of being followed. Of being watched.

He turned. Something red glittered in the darkness. Like hungry, glowing eyes.

They hadn't lost the vampires. The vampires were right behind him. The vampires were all around him.

They had Dawn. And now they were after him.

CHAPTER

11

"They got her," Martin repeated dully. "They got her."

"Do you have to keep saying that?" said Jeep. He looked over his shoulder. Sure enough, Pete was watching them.

Jeep smiled.

Pete smiled.

Jeep turned around and kept walking toward the canoes. He'd looked for Dawn at breakfast. But he hadn't been surprised when she hadn't turned up.

When Nora had seen him looking in her direction, she hadn't even giggled.

A bad sign. A very bad sign.

Martin said, "I just can't believe they got her. Did you see it happen? Was it awful?"

"No. I told you. One minute Dawn was there. The next minute she was gone. And that's when I knew there were vampires all around me."

"And you ran away."

"Well, what would you have done, Martin?" Martin was getting on Jeep's nerves. He was making Jeep feel guilty. *If he keeps it up,* Jeep thought, *I'm gonna feed him to the vampires.*

Aloud he said, "We have no other alternative. We have to run away—from here!"

"We do?"

"Martin. Think about it. What else can we do? They know who I am and what I know. They've probably guessed that you know, too. They're gonna come after us next."

"It's only two more days until camp is over," said Martin. "We could just be really careful. Take turns standing watch. Make some garlic necklaces."

"Have you seen any garlic around here?" asked Jeep. "Get real. We've got to make a run for it. Tonight. While we still can."

Martin's shoulders sagged. "You're right," he said.

Suddenly William said, "Hey, look who's back!" He waved wildly.

Lucian came bounding down the hill from the infirmary. "Wait for me!" he called.

Jeep shuddered and turned away.

"Did you see his teeth?" Martin gasped.

But by the time Lucian reached them, his smile revealed only his big, square front teeth. He was pale. But he was practically bursting with energy.

And he was wearing dark glasses.

"Hey, Lucian! Just in time to take a swim in the canoe!" William laughed loudly. Lucian laughed, too.

"You guys missed me, right?" he asked.

Jeep said, "Uh, sure."

"Glad you're feeling . . . you know," said Martin.

Lucian walked over to a canoe. He stood at one end, and William got at the other. But before William could even lift the canoe, Lucian had lifted practically the whole thing by himself, as if it weighed nothing at all.

"Wow," said William. "You're *definitely* feeling better."

"Superhuman strength," Martin whispered.

But Jeep wasn't listening. He was staring straight ahead. He couldn't believe his eyes. Dawn was casually walking toward him. Was it possible? Had Dawn escaped from the vampires?

He realized he was holding his breath as she came toward him. Would she be pale? Would her lips be stretched into a thin, weird smile to hide her newly grown fangs?

Dawn grinned. "How come you ran off and left me? Didja get scared?"

Immediately Jeep forgot he had *ever* worried about Dawn. His face turned red. "I didn't . . . you . . . I . . . ," he sputtered.

"You're alive?" asked Martin.

"Well, I'm not dead yet," answered Dawn.

"Campers, to your canoes," said Pete.

Dawn walked over to join Nora, who was frowning. She looked in Jeep's direction, then said something to Dawn.

"C'mon, Martin, time for our swim," said Jeep meanly, still annoyed at Dawn's accusation of cowardice. He grabbed his end of the canoe and began to drag it toward the lake.

"We did it, we did it!" Martin said. "We made it through a whole canoe lesson without turning over."

Stepping carefully out of the canoe, Martin bent to help Jeep pick it up and take it back up onto the shore.

"Way to go, Martin," William called.

"I know," said Martin proudly as he and Jeep maneuvered the canoe back into place with the other canoes.

Jeep cleared his throat. He straightened up. "Good work, Martin," he said, hoping he sounded normal.

He walked out to the end of the pier and sat down, letting his legs dangle over the edge. His feet, reflected in the dark water, looked enormous. A few minutes later Martin sat down on one side of him and crossed his legs under him. "I told Dawn we had a plan," he said. "She'll be here in a minute."

Jeep nodded. He stared out across the lake at the tree-ringed shore. Maybe they could steal a canoe and paddle to safety. But for some reason the thought of going out on the dark water of the lake by night made him shudder even more than the thought of wandering through the woods.

The trick in the woods would be to follow the road out—without getting caught. It wouldn't be easy. But the other choices were worse.

Dawn sat down on the other side of him. "So what's the plan?" she asked. They watched as the last of the canoers paddled by. The ripples broke up the distorted reflection of Jeep's huge feet. Martin's legs were folded up, so he couldn't see Martin's feet.

He couldn't see Dawn's feet, either.

Jeep glanced at Dawn. She had one leg folded under her. She was swinging the other over the edge of the pier. Back and forth her sneakered foot went. Back and forth.

The effect was hypnotic. Jeep forced himself to look away. To look back down into the gently rippling, glassy water.

His feet, his reflection, was the only one.

Dawn didn't have a reflection. Not anymore.

Then Jeep saw something else: the very end of a pair of dark glasses, stuck into the pocket of Dawn's denim vest.

Glasses just like the other vampires had been wearing.

It was true. The vampires had caught Dawn.

Dawn had become a vampire.

Quickly Jeep leaned back and folded his own legs up under him. He forced himself not to stare at Dawn's eyes. He was sure he would give himself away.

"We're going to make a break for it," Martin said. "We . . . owwww."

"Sorry," said Jeep. "My elbow slipped. Yeah, Martin and I've decided that we're going to steal a canoe and paddle across the lake and see if we can find a cabin with some people in it. Or even just a phone."

Dawn turned to look out over the lake. "I don't see any cabins," she said.

"It's our only chance," Martin explained solemnly. "We're going to leave to . . . owww!"

"I think I pulled a muscle in my arm last night," said Jeep smoothly. "Sorry, Martin. Yeah, tomorrow night. We're going to make a break for it tomorrow night."

"But . . . ," Martin began.

"Tomorrow," said Jeep firmly.

"Why not tonight?" said Dawn.

"Evidence," said Jeep. "We need to gather more evidence. What I think we should do is try to act as if we suspect nothing. I don't think they know who we are for sure yet."

Martin started to say something, glanced down at Jeep's elbow, and stopped.

"Then we meet tomorrow night after lights out, here on the pier. And we head out."

Dawn nodded. "I like it. It's simple. It could work. And if anybody can lead us back to civilization, it's me."

Elizabetta blew a shrill blast on her whistle. "Okay, boys and girls, let's hustle here."

"Later," said Dawn jumping to her feet and running down the pier.

"Yeah," agreed Jeep. Under his breath he added, "Like never."

"Jeep? What's going on?"

"She's a vampire," said Jeep flatly. "She didn't have a reflection in the lake. She's carrying a pair of dark glasses like all the senior campers wear."

"No," said Martin.

"Yes," said Jeep. "They did get her last night. And not only did they turn her into a vampire, they turned her into a *spy*."

The rest of the day crept by. Jeep knew he was being watched. He knew that every move he made, someone was watching. At the archery range he looked up and found Dawn staring at him from several yards away.

She raised her eyebrows.

Jeep pretended he hadn't seen.

His arrow thudded into the target next to his.

By dinnertime he was a mass of nerves. When Martin dropped his tray on the table next to Jeep, Jeep almost passed out from fright.

Martin ate with a huge appetite. Jeep pushed his food away.

"Hey, you're not eating." Martin looked surprised. Then a look of fear and suspicion crossed his face. "Why aren't you eating? You aren't . . . you haven't . . ."

"I'm just not hungry, okay?" Jeep snapped. "I can eat,

see?'' He crammed some bread into his mouth. He chewed. He swallowed.

He watched the others in the room watching.

I know who you are, he thought silently. *I'm not afraid.*

But it wasn't true. He was afraid. Very, very afraid.

And the worst part of the night was still ahead.

CHAPTER

12

William was asleep.

Was Lucian asleep? Jeep could hear the snorts and snores coming from William's bed.

But Lucian slept silently. Without moving. Without making a sound.

He slept like the dead.

Jeep yawned. He was so tired. So very tired. If he could just close his eyes for a minute. It had been an exhausting day. He'd had to act calm. Normal. Pretend he didn't know anything.

The dumb-camper act had almost killed him.

Martin had said he would stay awake, too. That was the plan, to stay awake until they were sure that everyone was asleep and then slip out and make the break to freedom.

Jeep's eyelids drooped.

Without realizing it, he fell asleep.

• • •

He awoke with a jerk sometime later. He didn't know how much later. But he knew it was late.

In the dark he waited, letting his eyes adjust to it. He could hear William's snorts and snores. He peered through the gloom at Lucian's bed.

But Lucian wasn't there.

Instinctively Jeep made a grab for his neck. But no vampires had been visiting him in the night while he slept. He was still safe.

He'd been lucky that time. But he and Martin couldn't afford to take any more chances. It was time to go. Time to make a break for it.

Jeep got slowly, cautiously, up off his creaky bunk. He tiptoed silently across the room.

William snored on.

He leaned over the dark figure on the bed. "Martin," he whispered.

Martin didn't answer.

"Martin," said Jeep.

Martin still didn't answer. It was a bad dream. A nightmare. One that he had been in before.

But it wasn't. It was real. Horribly real.

Before he even reached out to shake Martin, Jeep knew what had happened.

Martin had met a vampire.

I can still get away, thought Jeep wildly. *I can leave Martin and go for help. He doesn't have to be a vampire. They can help him. Get him counseling. Yeah, that's it. Aren't there guidance counselors out there?*

Career consultants? People who specialize in problems like this?

Jeep would never know. He must have made some sound. Done something to wake William up. Because the next thing he realized, bare feet were thudding across the cabin floor in the dark. And then the dim overhead lightbulb was switched on.

William stood there, staring sleepily at Jeep. "Wha'?" he yawned. He rubbed his eyes. Then he saw the expression on Jeep's face.

Wordlessly Jeep pointed at Martin.

William jumped back and held his hands out in front of him. "I don't want to catch it," he said.

"You can't," said Jeep. "Not unless they catch you." He stared sadly down at Martin's pale face.

William wasn't listening. "I'll go get Pete," he said. "Pete will know what to do!" William didn't seem to notice that Lucian wasn't there.

"I just bet he will," muttered Jeep.

As William blasted out of the cabin, Jeep bent forward. Martin's mouth was slightly open. Jeep squatted down. He stared at Martin's teeth.

No fangs. Not yet.

Jeep felt a surge of hope. Maybe Martin wasn't a vampire yet. Maybe there was still time to save him. And it was almost morning. The power of a vampire was weaker by day. If he could figure something out before tomorrow night, there might be hope for Martin still.

He heard voices. William and Pete were coming back. A third voice joined the first two.

"Hey, what's happening?"

It was Lucian. Lucian's voice went on. "I went to the bathroom. . . . Really? He caught it, too? Poor Martin."

Jeep felt his own lips draw back in a snarl. "Not yet," he whispered. "Not if I can help it."

It was the longest day of Jeep's life. He told himself over and over that his parents would be there tomorrow. All he had to do was hold out—hold out and save Martin.

He kept seeing himself reflected in the dark glasses of the campers and counselors. He looked pale. Almost as pale as *they* did. And jumpy. Definitely jumpy.

And it didn't help that everywhere he looked, dark glasses seemed to be turned in his direction. Watching him.

Around him the other campers ate their breakfast—or pretended to—and acted normal. But Jeep noticed that there were a lot more kids wearing dark glasses and looking unhealthily pale. Many, many more than the day before.

They outnumbered the real kids.

Then Jeep saw Dawn. She walked toward him.

Jeep wanted to cringe. He almost did.

The first words out of Dawn's mouth made him shudder. "Poor Martin," she said. "Poor, poor Martin." She looked around. She lowered her voice. "They got him, too, didn't they?"

"It looks like *they* did," Jeep said, unable to prevent himself from being sarcastic. "We'll just have to hold out until tomorrow. And be super careful."

"Is that the plan?" Dawn asked.

"You got any better ones?" asked Jeep. The old Dawn, the real Dawn, would have argued. Would have had about a million other plans.

She would have talked about rescuing Martin.

But not this Dawn. This Dawn nodded. "No, of course not. We'll just have to watch each other's backs. Trust each other."

"Trust each other," Jeep echoed. "Right."

"All for one and one for all," Dawn said.

"And every kid for themselves," muttered Jeep, watching Dawn glide away. Up at the front of the mess hall one of the counselors began making announcements about the awards ceremony that night. "We've all voted on these awards," she reminded the campers. "But I think there'll be some surprises, some nice surprises, too. So get psyched, everyone. Be there at the Campfire Circle after dinner. We want this to be a special night, one to remember. A real Camp Westerra event."

Jeep raised his head. He tried to look calm and unconcerned, but his thoughts were racing madly. Maybe he'd have a chance to rescue Martin after all. Maybe they could get out of Camp Westerra before it was too late.

He could do it that night while everyone was gathered for the awards ceremony. He could get Martin, and they

107

could make their escape. Even if they couldn't get away, they could hide until morning. Until their parents came.

The campers walked down the trail toward the Campfire Circle. Although it wasn't quite dark yet, some of the senior campers lined the path, holding flashlights and looking important—and sinister.

Jeep let himself lag farther and farther behind. Then he bent down and pretended to be tying his shoe.

He was pretty sure no one noticed when he slipped off the side of the trail and into the woods. He crouched in the underbrush watching the other campers go by. Some of them weren't wearing sunglasses. But most of them were now. And yet no one seemed to notice anything wrong with the picture.

Even though it was a warm night, Jeep shivered.

He waited until he was sure the last of the campers had gone by. He waited until the senior campers who had lined the trail had themselves gone up it to join the others for the awards ceremony at the Campfire Circle.

Then he scrambled out of his hiding place and ran back down the path toward the main camp area and the infirmary.

Compared with the last few times he'd run for his life through these woods, thought Jeep as he reached the infirmary and stopped, this was easy. A piece of cake.

Almost too easy.

Suddenly nervous, he looked over his shoulder. But no one was there. Everything was motionless, dark and still.

This time Jeep wasn't dumb enough to get caught going in the front door. He slid around and peered into the window near the front of the building. Sure enough, Nurse Hatchett was there. She was leaning back in a reclining chair in front of her television. Her head was tilted back. Her eyes were closed. She was snoring.

Cautiously Jeep went around to the other window. He straightened up and looked through the glass into the room where Lucian had been kept.

Martin was in the same bed Lucian had been in. The room was dark. The only light came from the hallway.

Without giving himself time to think about it, Jeep pried the window open and climbed quickly inside. As he landed, a weak voice said from the bed, "Who is it? Who's there?"

"Shhh! It's me, Martin. Jeep."

"Jeep?"

"Shhh! Yes. I've come to save you. You haven't spent a whole night here yet. I've got it figured out. They don't have any real power by day. At least not enough to do the vampire thing. I guess that's where having command over the animals helps. They can get the animals to keep an eye on things for them. But it's at night that you have to watch out."

"Is it nighttime?" Martin's voice sounded stronger. He sounded more like his old self.

"I'm gonna help you, Martin. We're gonna make a run for it. We . . ." Jeep had reached Martin's bed. His voice trailed off as Martin sat up.

Jeep took a step back. He opened his mouth. He tried to speak. But no sound would come out.

"It's nighttime," said Martin happily. He turned toward Jeep. The dark glasses he was wearing glinted in the faint light.

"You like 'em?" Martin said. "Of course I don't really need them at night, but they're pretty decently cool, don't you think, Jeep?"

"They got you," Jeep whispered hoarsely. "They got you, too!"

Martin smiled. His fangs looked very sharp.

"No way!" screamed Jeep. He turned and flung himself toward the window.

But Martin wasn't slow and clumsy anymore. Somehow he got there before Jeep. He blocked the window. "What's wrong, Jeep?" he asked. "Aren't we friends anymore?"

With a mindless shriek Jeep turned and ran for the door. Nurse Hatchett stepped out in the hall as he ran by. He felt her hand on his arm. But he dodged out from under it and burst out the door of the infirmary.

His plan was to start running—and never stop.

There was just one problem with the plan.

The large crowd of vampires that was waiting outside the door when he ran out.

CHAPTER
13

Jeep skidded to a stop.

They were all there. The whole camp. Every single person.

They were all wearing dark glasses. They were all smiling. Behind him Jeep heard footsteps come out of the infirmary door. He looked over his shoulder. Nurse Hatchett and Martin were standing there. Nurse Hatchett had on her dark glasses, too. And she and Martin were both smiling vampire smiles.

"Stand back!" screamed Jeep. "I had garlic for dinner!"

No one spoke. No one moved. They just stood there watching Jeep.

Hungrily.

Then Dawn stepped out. She pushed her sunglasses up. Her pale face glowed in the dark. "Garlic for dinner, Jeep? I don't think so. You see, we don't serve garlic at this camp."

The other vampires came closer. Closer. He was surrounded on every side. He pulled the collar of his shirt up. He put up his fists. He closed his eyes.

"You'll never take me alive!" he cried.

And someone began to laugh.

Then someone else laughed. Then more people joined in.

Jeep opened his eyes.

A porch light came on behind him, flooding the scene with brightness. The campers and counselors began to take off their dark glasses. Dawn reached up and pulled something out of her mouth. She stuck out her hand. Two wax fangs lay on her palm.

Now everyone was laughing.

Jeep blinked. "What is this?" he asked. "Some kind of a dumb joke?"

"Gotcha!" shouted Martin. "We really had you, didn't we, Jeep?"

"This was a *joke*? A big, dumb practical joke? This whole thing?" Jeep was outraged.

"Please, please don't turn me into a vampire," said William, and doubled over with laughter.

"You're not all vampires. You're not going to turn me into a—"

"—a vampire!" Dawn shrieked, finishing for Jeep. She laughed hysterically, maniacally. "Sure we are, Jeep. And after that we're all going to teach you how to fly like a bat."

Jeep stood there as the waves of laughter washed over

him. He was furious. He couldn't believe he'd fallen for it all.

He couldn't believe they'd done that to him.

Mr. Renfield stepped forward. He gave Jeep a hearty pat on the shoulder. "A bit of fun we have with new campers. You've been a good sport, Jeep. Let's get back to the awards ceremony."

The director turned and raised his arms. His cloak swirled out around him. "Let's give Jeep a big hand for being such a good sport," said Mr. Renfield.

Jeep looked around. He forced himself to smile. What else could he do?

Amid applause he turned and headed back toward the Campfire Circle.

Behind him he heard the director announce, "And after the awards we'll have a special treat for everyone. Pizza—with garlic—at the mess hall!"

"Yeahhhhh," said Martin. "I'm starved." He bounded down the path and fell into step next to Jeep. "You aren't mad, are you, Jeep? I got the idea when I saw those bats. They were just ordinary bats, but you were so freaked about them that I just couldn't help it."

"You thought of all this?" said Jeep, staring at Martin. "You?"

"All in the Camp Westerra tradition of good, clean fun," intoned Mr. Renfield from behind them.

"Good, clean fun," repeated Jeep. "You call this fun?"

Dawn walked up to join Jeep and Martin.

Behind them Jeep heard Nora giggle.

He heard Dawn sigh.

Then Martin said, "Uh, Jeep? Here. I have a present for you." He held out his hand. In the palm was a pair of sunglasses.

His parents' station wagon came lurching over the ruts in the parking lot of Camp Westerra. For once in their lives they were early.

And a good thing, too, thought Jeep.

"Mom! Dad! Over here!" he called, waving wildly.

His parents got out of the car. His father came up and grabbed Jeep's duffel bag. His mother hugged Jeep and ruffled his hair.

A heavy hand fell on Jeep's shoulder. He knew without turning that it was Mr. Renfield. "Your son is an excellent sport. He has the makings of a fine camper."

Both of Jeep's parents looked surprised and a little amused. Mrs. Holmes said, "Well, Jeep. I thought you hated the whole idea of camp. You changed your mind?"

Jeep shrugged. "It wasn't so bad."

Mr. Holmes had stowed Jeep's duffel bag in the car. He and Mrs. Holmes shook hands with Mr. Renfield.

Jeep got into the car. He waved at Martin. As the car pulled away, he saw Dawn come charging up to the parking lot. She waved, too. "Hey, Jeep," she shouted. "Watch out for *bats!*"

"Ha, ha!" Jeep shouted back, hanging his head out

the window. Then the car pulled around the first curve in the road, and the camp was gone from sight.

They drove in silence for a few miles until they'd passed beneath the big gate marking the entrance to the camp. Then Mrs. Holmes turned and faced Jeep. "Report?" she said.

Jeep cleared his throat. "They're definitely vampires," he said. "A whole campful in various stages of the vampire cycle. But it's like a real camp. I mean, they do real camp things just like anybody else. By day as well as by night."

Mrs. Holmes nodded. "The new sunscreens that are on the market. Unbelievable."

"Give you any trouble?" Jeep's father asked, glancing into his rearview mirror. Apparently he didn't see anything to worry about. He kept driving at the same easy pace.

Jeep made a face. He didn't want to admit that he *had* been scared. "Not too much. I had my garlic vampire repellant with me. They played some pretty dumb tricks on me, though. One of them actually had me fooled there for a while. I thought he was some innocent bystander who'd wandered into the camp by mistake." Jeep thought of Martin and smiled. "He was excellent."

"Not surprising," said Jeep's mother. "By the way, your letters were very well done. Nice use of code. We'll want a full debriefing when we get back to headquarters. But meanwhile, well done, son."

"Thanks," said Jeep. "So, what's the plan now? We go in, we wipe them out?"

"Wipe them out?" Mrs. Holmes shook her head. "Of course not! We're not barbarians. We don't kill others just because they are different. In the old days, of course, it was war, vampires against the humans. But we simply engage in the peaceful monitoring of their activities."

Mr. Holmes added, "As long as they don't bother us and rely on the new synthetic food sources. You know, son, we're all in it together, here on this planet."

Jeep leaned back. "Good grief," he complained. But secretly he was sort of glad. He'd liked Martin. And maybe Dawn, too. Sort of.

Even if they were vampires.

"Do you think we fooled him?" asked Martin. Now the rest of the camp had come to join Dawn and Martin and Mr. Renfield in the parking lot. Everyone was wearing their dark glasses. The smell of super sunscreen was heavy in the air. It was a bright and sunny day.

Mr. Renfield pushed back his pith helmet. He said thoughtfully, "I kind of doubt that. But you two did a good job. In fact, you all did. We got a lot of good information about modern humans and their vampire-related prejudices and activities. . . . You're all going to grow up to be excellent vampires."

William said, "Except Lucian. He almost gave the whole thing away, turning into a giant rat and following Jeep around."

"So I got a little carried away," retorted Lucian "I covered my tracks. It turned out okay."

Dawn shook her head. "Humans will believe anything. Can you get over it?"

Martin said, "Hey, Jeep was okay. And besides, I really *don't* like garlic."

"That's because you're weird," said Dawn.

"Now, now, you two," said the director. "That's enough." He turned to the rest of the campers. "We have plenty of time yet left to enjoy camp, have fun. Let's make the most of it. Everyone head back to their cabins and get some rest." He paused. He raised his arms. He smiled and the sun glinted off his fangs.

"The night will be here before you know it."

Vampire Word Search!

Find the following words in the puzzle below. Hint: Words can go up, down, diagonally, forward, and backward, too!

Fang	Blood
Garlic	Vampire
Coffin	Fright
Stake	Dirt
Bat	Pale

```
C  F  R  I  G  H  T  Y
V  A  M  P  I  R  E  E
F  N  K  V  A  N  R  L
E  G  A  R  L  I  C  T
W  B  S  I  P  F  A  R
A  L  T  M  A  F  R  I
H  O  A  B  L  O  O  D
U  V  K  A  E  C  K  A
J  D  E  T  Q  U  E  T
```

Laugh
TILL YOU
Scream!

With each and every one of these scary, creepy, delightfully, frightfully funny books, you'll be dying to go to the *Graveyard School!*

Order any or all of the books in this scary new series by **Tom B. Stone**! Just check off the titles you want, then fill out and mail the order form below.

☐	0-553-48223-8	**DON'T EAT THE MYSTERY MEAT!**	$3.50/$4.50 Can.
☐	0-553-48224-6	**THE SKELETON ON THE SKATEBOARD**	$3.50/$4.50 Can.
☐	0-553-48225-4	**THE HEADLESS BICYCLE RIDER**	$3.50/$4.50 Can.
☐	0-553-48226-2	**LITTLE PET WEREWOLF**	$3.50/$4.50 Can.
☐	0-553-48227-0	**REVENGE OF THE DINOSAURS**	$3.50/$4.50 Can.

Bantam Doubleday Dell
Books For Young Readers

BDD BOOKS FOR YOUNG READERS
2451 South Wolf Road
Des Plaines, IL 60018

Please send me the items I have checked above. I am enclosing $_____
(please add $2.50 to cover postage and handling).
Send check or money order, no cash or C.O.D.s please.

NAME _____

ADDRESS _____

CITY _____ STATE _____ ZIP _____

Please allow four to six weeks for delivery.
Prices and availability subject to change without notice.   BFYR 113 2/95